Suicidal Date

Part Three of the "**Suicidal**" book trilogy.

S A M M Y   J O
D A N C E Y

The EC Publishing LLC books may be ordered
through booksellers or by contacting:

EC Publishing LLC
116 South Magnolia Ave.
Suite 3, Unit F
Ocala, FL 34471, USA
Direct Line: +1 (352) 644-6538
Fax: +1 (800) 483-1813
http://www.ecpublishingllc.com/

Ordering Information:
Quantity sales. Special discounts are available on quantity purchases by corporations, associations, and others. For details, contact the publisher at the address above.

Printed in the United States of America

This book is earnestly dedicated to the brave souls of Law Enforcement, the dedicated First Responders who rush into the chaos, and the esteemed Veterans of the Armed Forces. Your unwavering courage and sacrifice inspire the pages that follow.

Acknowledgements

The author wholeheartedly acknowledges the individuals listed below for their crucial role in shaping her into the therapist she is today. Their contributions have been vital to her development and success in this field.

- Gary & Sue Stockton - Phoenix Heroes CIC

- Ollie Smith – 42 Commando Royal Marines

- Helen Priestley – Devon & Cornwall Police

- 42 Commando Royal Marines & Avon & Somerset Police

- Chris Burnell – 1st Battalion, Royal Anglian Regiment

- Stewart Henderson BEM – Scots Guards & Parliamentary and Diplomatic Protection Group, Metropolitan Police

- Darren Sherwin – Grenadier Guards

- Emma Paddison – Former Military Wife, VAWG & DV Survivor

- Dean Owen – No Duff UK CIC

- Dan Johnson – Royal Engineers & Specialist Firearms Officer, Cheshire & Merseyside Police

- Nigel Oseman – West Midlands Police

- Kian Brady (1976–2021) – *The Hineycombe Bitch*, and a dearly missed friend

Contents

Chapter 1

2019

An instructor at SCO19 (Specialist Operations, Firearms & Counter Terrorism Command) emailed, asking her to be their in-house therapist. She was delighted and emailed back immediately with her terms; she was mid-range for a counsellor. In London, you can pay anywhere between £100 and £200 per session.

Her only concern was Sox & Paws, her beautiful cats, and what she would do with them if she had to be in Kent for three days a week. The instructor offered for her to take them with her, but they were not good at travelling and did not like to be left on their own for long periods.
Sox had become restless and destructive; the move back to the apartment had upset him as he could no longer roam outside. Sammy could see it was making him psychologically unwell. He had a wild look in his eye and would meow in distress at her constantly. He clawed at the door, the window frames, and furniture with a passion.

Sammy knew what she had to do.

Tentatively, she called Cats Protection and made enquiries about having Sox re-homed somewhere with a garden or lots of land. It wasn't long before a suitable home on a farm in the Dorset countryside was found for him. It was for the best, seeing him so stressed and cooped up was so upsetting.

He had been her loyal companion for twelve long years, and her affection for him was boundless. Yet, deep down, she sensed his unease; he was a soul yearning for freedom—the kind that allowed him to roam far and wide like a wild tomcat. He longed to hunt, to chase the fluttering birds and scurrying mice, and to mark out his territory with the unmistakable scent of tomcat urine, a potent aroma that clung to everything it touched. She winced at the thought of him leaving his musky mark on the furniture, a smell that could invade every corner of their home.

He also needed the companionship of female cats. His sister, Paws, was often indifferent, swatting him away if he dared to approach her for affection, leaving him looking utterly lost and forlorn in his quest for connection. She could sense the longing in his eyes, the desire for companionship that extended beyond their years of friendship, and it broke her heart to watch him suffer in silence.

The dreaded day arrived, casting a heavy shadow over her heart. With trembling hands, she gently placed him inside the cat carrier, carefully tucking in a couple of his beloved toys and a soft pillowcase infused with her familiar scent. As she drove toward Cats Protection, the world outside seemed to blur into an indistinct haze, mirroring the tumult of emotions swirling within her.

With a composed exterior, she handed him over, yet the moment felt like a betrayal; her legs quaked beneath her as if they might collapse at any second. An unbearable weight settled in her chest, squeezing tightly as she whispered her heartfelt wishes for his future, forcing the words past the lump in her throat. Tears escaped her eyes, cascading down her cheeks like a gentle rain, as she slowly turned away, each step back to her car feeling like an insurmountable distance. The drive home felt interminable, the silence amplifying her sorrow, echoing her profound sense of loss.

Paws sat patiently in her favourite spot on the high bookshelf in the dimly lit hallway, gazing down as Sammy approached. With trembling hands, Sammy picked her up, cradling the fluffy little cat tightly against her chest while tears streamed down her cheeks. She sobbed deeply, heartbroken and heavy with guilt, even though a part of her understood that she had made the right decision.

Nights turned into weeks filled with sorrow. Sammy would lie in bed, the weight of her loss crushing her as she longed for the gentle purring and warm cuddles that Sox had always provided. Each sound in the empty apartment seemed to echo her feelings of loneliness, amplifying her heartbreak.

Paws seemed to thrive in her newfound independence. With her elder brother gone, she was relieved of daily annoyances—no more sharing her litter tray with an unwelcome companion, and no more worrying about someone sneaking bites of her food when she wasn't looking. She roamed freely around the apartment, basking in the sunlight that streamed through the window and finding cozy spots to nap without interruption.

Whenever Sammy settled down on the couch, Paws would nimbly leap onto her lap, seeking affection. However, those moments now carried a bittersweet nostalgia, reminding her of the bond she once shared with Sox.

Over time, both Sammy and Paws began to adapt to their changed circumstances in different ways. Sammy learned to embrace the memories of their adventures together, holding onto the joyful moments while gradually finding ways to fill the void left behind. Meanwhile, Paws revelled in her solitude but still seemed to keep an eye on Sammy, as if sensing her lingering sadness.

Although grief is a heavy burden, time has a way of healing wounds, and their individual journeys allowed them to move forward, carrying cherished memories while discovering new paths in life.

The SCO19 instructor reached out, providing her with client details and authorising 12 coaching sessions.

"I just want to give you a brief heads-up about her," he suggested, his tone hinting at his concern.

Yet, she knew all too well the pitfalls of basing her perspective on someone else's account of a client's struggles. Such narratives often came wrapped in hearsay and tainted by judgments, misunderstandings, and personal biases. She preferred to start fresh, armed only with her own observations, ready to dive deep into the client's unique truth.

As she pressed the digits of the number he had given her, a rush of anticipation surged through her, fluttering in her chest like a bird testing its wings. She could almost sense the weight of her client's emotions resting on the line, heavy and unresolved, as she waited for the connection to be made.

When the client finally answered, the sorrow in her voice hung thick in the air, akin to a dense fog that enveloped the surroundings. Sammy leaned in closer, her heart attuned to the fragile tones of her client's words as she began to unfold her story. Each detail poured out like water from a long-turned tap, seeking the solace and understanding that only this moment could provide.

This client, a dedicated officer for 18 gruelling years, had faced countless traumatic scenes, but none had pierced her heart like the tragic sight of a woman leaping from a bridge before her eyes. That haunting image lingered in her mind, casting a shadow over her spirit and pushing her to seek the healing they might uncover together.

The officer had desperately tried to reach her, using words in an earnest bid to save her life, but in a heartbreaking moment, she leaped, and she stood frozen, a witness to the despair unfurling before her. This tragic scene struck deep at her sense of humanity, leaving her utterly shaken. It eroded her resilience, making her grapple with profound questions about her own mortality, her faith, and the direction of her life.

For 12 weeks, Sammy and her client engaged in regular weekly sessions, weaving a tapestry of trust and understanding. As their meetings progressed, the barriers began to dissolve, and slowly, the client peeled back layers of her guarded heart, revealing the vulnerabilities within.

Donning a uniform and embodying the role of a rescuer is a formidable task. It demands immense courage and unwavering resilience. Officers are often thrust into the grim realities of life, where they confront the darkest corners of humanity: suicides that shatter families, homicides that leave communities in shock, the haunting stories of sexual assault and child abuse, and the violence that scars lives. The aftermath of road traffic collisions paints a particularly grim picture. Over time, these harrowing experiences weigh heavily on the soul.

Sammy was acutely aware that each officer was a complex individual beneath the polished exterior of their uniform, not merely a machine programmed to respond to emergencies. They navigate their own private lives, filled with the joy of family, the pain of illness, the strain of financial worries, the affection for their pets, and the daily stresses that everyone faces. Each officer carries their own burdens, crafting an intricate blend of bravery and vulnerability.

It is entirely natural to be impacted by trauma; this is what defines our humanity. Yet, there exists an unspoken expectation that officers must remain unflinching, able to withstand the unimaginable. This pressure makes it incredibly difficult for them to voice their struggles when they are deeply affected.

She sat quietly, absorbing her client's stories of the vivid horrors witnessed over 18 long years in the line of duty. The officer recounted heart-wrenching scenes: families shattered and left in turmoil, the stark reality of death looming large, the acrid smells of anguish lingering in the air, the bitter taste of fear that hung heavily on her tongue, and the gut-wrenching sounds of screams echoing in her mind. She spoke of the agonising moment of delivering a death notification, when she would witness the bewildered, haunted look in a family member's eyes, a gaze that said more than words ever could.

They both sat quietly, the air thick with tension, until Sammy broke the stillness. Her voice was steady but gentle as she turned to her client, "Are you having thoughts of suicide?"

The answer came reluctantly. "Yes," her client admitted, vulnerability flickering in their eyes, "The incident was in the local newspaper."

Sammy, feeling a weight settle in her chest, asked carefully, "Do you mind if I read it now?"

"Go ahead," her client replied, a hint of resignation in their tone.

With a sense of urgency mixed with compassion, Sammy pulled out her phone, her fingers dancing across the screen as she searched for the article. When she finally found it, she took a deep breath and began to read, the words unfolding the painful story that had brought them to this moment.

The family of a 22-year-old woman from Cornwall, who tragically died after jumping from the Tamar Bridge, has expressed their gratitude to the police officers who endeavoured to save her life.

At around 11:30pm on 7th July of the previous year, two officers attempted to persuade the woman to return to safety as she stood precariously on the scaffolding outside the bridge's railings. Despite their efforts, she let go and fell 95 feet, suffering fatal head injuries upon landing on Old Ferry Road on the Saltash side of the River Tamar.

During the coroner's inquest held at County Hall in Truro, her parents, grandmother, and brother extended their thanks to the officers involved in the incident.

The inquest revealed that the young woman had been struggling with long-standing mental health issues and had previously made several attempts to take her own life. Since 2010, she had been admitted to emergency care 58 times due to overdoses and self-harming behaviours. Medical professionals had diagnosed her with anxiety, depression, post-traumatic stress disorder (PTSD), obsessive-compulsive disorder (OCD), and emotionally unstable personality disorder. On the day of her death, she had taken an overdose and inflicted injuries on her wrists.

Witnesses reported that a member of the public alerted the police after discovering her on the scaffolding poles below the pedestrian walkway and beyond the safety barrier of the bridge.

The first responding officer, an inspector, noted that the woman was situated two metres beyond the safety barrier on the scaffolding, emphasising that it would have been unsafe for anyone to attempt to reach her. Shortly thereafter, two additional officers from Liskeard arrived on the scene. One officer ascended to the bridge while the other went below to close Old Ferry Road.

The inspector and the second officer recounted their attempts to communicate with the woman as they awaited the arrival of a police negotiator and a fire service rope team. They faced challenges due to the loud traffic noise and requested that the bridge be closed to improve conditions for engagement.

Throughout their conversation, the woman expressed a firm belief that no one could help her, stating, "Yes, but you won't get me to change my mind." Despite their appeals for her to move away from the edge, she remained unresponsive and ultimately became agitated, leading the officers to step back. In that moment, she pushed herself off the edge.

Reflecting on the situation, the responding officer stated, "We couldn't reach where she was at all. I felt shocked." The inspector expressed deep regret over the incident, saying, "I immediately felt sick. We always approach such

situations intending to help, and this time that did not happen."

The inquest concluded with the coroner's findings that the woman died from head injuries sustained from the fall, recording a verdict of suicide while suffering from mental illness. In response to this tragedy, signs have been installed at either end of the bridge encouraging individuals in distress to contact the Samaritans. Additionally, a review of mental health services in Plymouth has been conducted, with findings shared with the relevant services in Cornwall. Although the inquest determined that nothing could have prevented her death, seven critical lessons regarding the treatment of patients have been identified for future improvement.

Her client sighed deeply.

"We couldn't save her, and it was so horrifying to watch her fall," she whispered, her voice trembling.

Sammy listened patiently, allowing her client to express her feelings before gently holding a moment of silence.

"How could she do that to her family? Those poor people will never get over this," the client continued, her eyes filled with sadness.

"They will find a way to heal," Sammy said softly, her tone reassuring. "People are incredibly resilient. The pain is immense, but the capacity for recovery is even greater. You did everything you could. I relate to your experience; my brother Ian took his life in 1984, and I still remember the impact it had on all of us. It's understandable to feel survivor's guilt. I'd like to send you a worksheet to help you navigate these feelings. How does that sound?"

"Yes, that sounds helpful. Thank you, Sam. I'll talk to you next week."

"Remember, if you need me before then, don't hesitate to reach out. I'm here for you," Sammy said with warmth and compassion.

Over a span of three months, they engaged in 12 transformative sessions of Cognitive Behavioural Therapy, delving deep into their thoughts and emotions. Following a thorough evaluation by the Force Medical Officer and a psychiatrist, the officer faced a significant turning point in their life; they received a diagnosis of Complex Post-Traumatic Stress Disorder and retired. This realisation marked the beginning of a new chapter, as the weight of their experiences became acknowledged and understood.

Sammy often found herself behind the wheel of Miss Scarlett, her vibrant red Alfa Romeo, with the wind tousling her hair as the roof folded down.

After a particularly tumultuous encounter that left her rattled, she craved the solace of the open road to help her regain her footing in the present moment.

As she sat idling in front of the gates of her apartment complex, the warm rays glinting off the sleek curves of her car, a cheerful figure caught her eye. He was a friendly-looking guy, casually donning a faded Boston Red Sox baseball cap. His smile was inviting as he ambled toward her, and she could almost hear the soft purr of the engine matching the rhythm of their brief connection.

"Prrrrr...... Kitty Kitty, nice car!"

She immediately recognised the charming Irish lilt in his voice, a melodic accent that evoked warmth and familiarity. A smile spread across her face as she drove away, her mind wandering with curiosity about him—was he merely passing through this place, or was he a resident, woven into the fabric of the community?

A couple of days later, fate brought them together once more, this time on foot. They crossed paths near the elegant concierge's office, the sunlight casting a soft glow around them, the air filled with the gentle hum of beach life.

"Hello again, Kitty!" he exclaimed, his tone warm and inviting.

"Hi! Do you live here?" Sammy inquired, a spark of curiosity dancing in her eyes.

"Yes, I reside in the penthouse on the corner," he replied with a hint of pride, a smile playing at the corners of his lips.

"Sammy, pleased to meet you," she said, extending her hand with genuine enthusiasm.

"Kian, a pleasure to meet you too," he responded, his grip firm and friendly as they shook hands.

"How about we grab a drink?" she suggested, her smile brightening the space between them as she noticed the glimmer of excitement in his eyes.

"Sure, I'd love to! Let's head to my place," Kian said, his voice brimming with eagerness.

They clicked instantly. Sammy had always been captivated by the Irish; their melodic accent stirred something profound within her, perhaps a hint of her Celtic heritage, as she proudly claimed Scottish roots with her mother hailing from the vibrant city of Glasgow.

After collecting her parcel from the concierge office, they ascended to Kian's apartment, where a breathtaking sight awaited her. The view stretched magnificently from west to east, showcasing the shimmering waters of Swanage and the distant silhouette of the Isle of Wight. Perched high above the bustling promenade, the sounds of lively chatter were lost to the wind, replaced by the powerful, rhythmic roar of the ocean crashing against the shore.

The balcony was nothing short of extraordinary—the largest she had ever encountered among all the penthouses. It was elegantly furnished with a table and chairs, inviting leisurely meals under the sun, alongside plush sun loungers perfect for soaking up the warmth and taking in the stunning panorama.

"Wine?" Kian asked, his voice warm and inviting as he strolled towards the imposing American-style fridge that gleamed like a beacon in the kitchen.

"Red, please. I don't drink white," Sammy replied, feeling a flutter of anticipation.

"Not a problem at all! Are you hungry? I used to be a chef on the QE2," he said, giving her a playful wink that revealed a charming sparkle in his brown eyes.

"Sure, I could use a bite," she answered, a smile spreading across her face. Wow, she thought, what an intriguing guy.

With a friendly grin, he reassured her, "I am gay, so there's no need to worry. You're quite safe here."

She couldn't help but notice how warm and gentle his gaze was, framed by thick lashes that contrasted with the baldness of his head. His impressive, bushy beard added a rugged charm, and she was struck by the whimsical thought that he resembled a playful leprechaun.

They settled onto the balcony, the soft evening breeze around them as they looked out over the shimmering bay, where the water sparkled like a thousand tiny diamonds under the setting sun. Sammy, her eyes dancing with excitement, raised her glass and proclaimed with a beaming smile, "Well, no good story ever started with a salad, did it? Cheers!"

In that moment filled with laughter and clinking glasses, it was clear this was the beginning of a firm and cherished friendship.

Chapter 2

Private Practice

"So, what do you do for work?" Kian inquired, his voice filled with curiosity as he savoured his mimosa, the sunlight sparkling off the balcony that he affectionately dubbed the deck.

"I specialise as a PTSD therapist," Sammy responded, her tone earnest and passionate. "I provide support to police officers and veterans. I recently completed my qualifications with CPCAB and proudly became a member of the British Association for Counselling and Psychotherapy. However, my journey as a PTSD practitioner began back in 2012, and I've dedicated myself to working with armed forces veterans and the brave men and women in law enforcement ever since."

Kian's eyes sparkled at the revelation. "Oh, how fascinating! I don't hail from Northern Ireland; I'm actually from the picturesque town of Cavan in the south, where my family runs a charming farm. But I spent years working aboard the QE2, and let me tell you, I have some incredible stories to share with you, Sammy!"

His laughter erupted like a warm wave, filling the air with a contagious joy as he poured them both another glass.

"Look over there on that cabinet; that's my cherished memorabilia from my time on the crew. It was an adventure filled with vibrant experiences! I even had the thrill of meeting Tom Jones! The work was demanding, though—it could either uplift your spirit or break you down. How about I whip up a meal for us later? You're more than welcome to stay, my dear Bournemouth sister. These days, I work at a lovely local restaurant right by the beach. On sunny days, I enjoy taking a leisurely walk there, but most of the time, I treat myself to a taxi ride; I have an account with them. Cooking brings me joy, and the atmosphere there is incredibly inviting," he continued with a grin. "I do have a driver's license, but honestly, I can't be bothered to buy a car."

"I can give you a lift if you'd like," Sammy offered, her voice warm and inviting. "I'm always up early, and the morning drives are my favourite. The fresh air clears my mind, and the breathtaking views from the Overcliff never fail to take my breath away. We're so fortunate to call this place home," she glanced out towards the horizon, where the sun kissed the sea.

Kian's eyes lit up with enthusiasm. "You must come out to the farm in Cavan! My parents would absolutely adore meeting you. They're visiting soon,

and it would be the perfect time for you to join us.
I make it back home frequently whenever I get the
chance," he said, an excited glimmer dancing in his
eyes.

Sammy turned to gaze across the bay, soaking
in the warmth of the sun and the gentle caress
of the breeze against her skin. The light buzz
from the wine had wrapped her in a comforting
glow, making her feel at ease in Kian's delightful
company. "I would love that!" she exclaimed,
a bright smile lighting up her face as she
affectionately referred to him as her 'Bournemouth
Brother.' She couldn't help but think about the
name Kian, how it closely echoed that of her
brother Ian.

Kian raised his glass in a toast, the sunlight
catching the amber liquid as he and Sammy clinked
their glasses together in a joyful cheer. "Sláinte!"
they proclaimed in unison, their voices mingling
with the sounds of the gentle waves lapping at the
shore.

"I have the luxury of taking Mondays off, especially
since the restaurant buzzes with life and energy all
weekend long. But after I wrap up my shift around
5pm on Sunday, I'm all yours for a good drink if
you're free," he said with a grin, his eyes sparkling
with anticipation.

Kian refilled his glass, the ice clinking rhythmically as he probed her with curious questions.

"Funny enough, I also find myself free on Mondays, which makes Sunday night perfect for a little escapade," she replied, her voice light, a hint of mischief dancing in her tone.

Sammy eagerly raised her glass, inviting Kian to pour more liquid courage into it. As they clinked their glasses, a shared exhilaration took over, and together they burst into an impromptu rendition of The Boomtown Rats, their voices intertwining in joyful harmony.

"Tell me why, I don't like Mondays!"

"Have you been keeping busy with clients lately?" he inquired, his brow slightly furrowed in genuine interest.

"It's a peaceful moment right now, just the three clients. I've been busy tirelessly crafting the foundation of my business. I'm officially registered as self-employed with HMRC, and I've made sure to secure proper insurance and align myself with a reputable regulating body, like the British Association for Counselling and Psychotherapy (BACP), which guarantees that I operate within ethical boundaries. I've also registered with the Information Commissioners Office to ensure compliance with GDPR, and I've even launched a website to showcase my services," Sammy shared, a spark of pride in her voice.

"You could counsel me; I really need therapy!" Kian laughed heartily, his voice breaking the calm ambiance.

"Doesn't everyone? But ethically, I can't offer you that kind of help because we're friends. It's against the guidelines to counsel anyone I have a personal relationship with," Sammy replied, her expression shifting to one of sincerity.

"Oh, I didn't know that. Shite!" he exclaimed, pulling a playful face that blended surprise with a touch of embarrassment.

"Most people get their ideas from movies or dramatic TV shows, which often misrepresent how things really are," Sammy explained, her lips curving into a wry smile, emphasising the absurdity of common misconceptions.

"So, how long have you lived here?" he inquired, his curiosity evident.

"Eight years, and I'll hit the nine-year mark in January. I absolutely love it here! It's the best decision I've ever made. The tranquility is enchanting, and every night, the gentle sound of the ocean lulls me to sleep; it's incredibly soothing. I can only imagine how much louder it must be right on the water," she replied, a smile gracing her lips as she looked out at the waves.

"Oh, how thoughtless of me! I haven't given you a proper tour yet, Sammy. Come on, let me show you around!" he exclaimed, his enthusiasm contagious as he motioned for her to follow.

Sammy stepped into the master bedroom, her breath catching in her throat at the sight before her. It was a sanctuary of luxury, boasting a private balcony that framed a breathtaking view of the sparkling sea. The en-suite bathroom was nothing short of opulent, sprawling out like a mini oasis with a deep soaking tub that seemed to beckon her to unwind. A sleek TV was cleverly integrated into the wall above the tub, while an array of mirrors danced across the opposite wall, creating a mesmerising sense of space and light. The shower was enormous, promising a refreshing escape with its spacious design.

As they continued their tour, they entered the second bedroom, equally impressive with its own intimate balcony and en-suite bathroom. The room exuded comfort, with mirrored wardrobes that gleamed and reflected the soft light, stretching along one wall, while a plush double bed sat invitingly in the middle, adorned with luxurious linens.

Kian gestured toward a small door. "There's another WC right here that you can use. And that room over there, I call 'The Press.' It's where I hang the laundry and store things. Not that I handle the laundry myself, of course; I leave that to the cleaners," he explained, his tone casual yet confident.

"I wouldn't trust them at all," Sammy warned, her brow furrowing in concern. "I've already lodged an official complaint about their incessant gossip and rude demeanour. It's not just hearsay; they have a reputation for charging unsuspecting customers twice for the same piece of work. I urge you to tread carefully, Kian. You really can't rely on them," her eyes, filled with a mix of worry and determination, locked onto his, emphasising the seriousness of her words.

"Oh, feck! They struck me as quite peculiar," he exclaimed, his eyes wide with surprise and a hint of disbelief colouring his tone.

"I will not give them access to my property; they are likely to rummage through all my belongings," Sammy was resolute.

"Michael, that's his name," Sammy began, her eyes narrowing slightly. "He was gossiping to me about a resident's personal affairs, completely oblivious to the fact that we're friends. I was really annoyed. I still remember attending a residents' meeting back in 2011 with my neighbour, and guess who was there? Why on earth would he show up at a residents' meeting?" A look of confusion crossed her face.

Kian leaned in, a mischievous grin spreading across his face. "That's bizarre! He must have been snooping. He sounds worse than us queens; we thrive on a good bit of gossip! Maybe he's a closeted gay man, and his wife is so heavy because she drowns her anger in food. In fact, she's so large that she could have sat next to everyone in high school without a second thought!" He erupted into laughter, a loud, infectious cackle that ended with a snort, causing him to dissolve into even more laughter.

Sammy couldn't help but join him, collapsing into a fit of giggles. She revelled in the playful wickedness of gay banter; it was utterly hilarious and completely irresistible.

"Ohhhh Bitchy Ki Ki!!" Sammy giggled.

"Oh didn't ye know, I AM the Hineycombe Bitch!"

With a burst of energy, he leaped to his feet, filling the air with lively tunes as he cranked up the music. The deck transformed into his personal stage as he grooved, every movement radiating joy. It was a mesmerising sight, watching him sing and dance along to "Shiny Disco Balls," his laughter ringing out melodically against the backdrop of shimmering lights.

"I lodged an official complaint with PMB Property Management about Michael after his audacious attempt to control my choices. As I strolled through the parking lot, he confronted me, claiming, "He's after your money," regarding a relationship I was in. I was taken aback by his boldness. Even more shocking was his insistence that I should abstain from drinking with my friends. I was stunned and momentarily speechless. My two friends were excitedly visiting for the weekend, and as I stepped through the door holding a bottle of wine, he unleashed another judgmental comment: "You shouldn't be drinking; you're not very nice when you've been drinking," his words hung in the air, heavy with unwarranted criticism, leaving me feeling both bewildered and angry.

I was completely taken aback, disbelief washing over me like a cold wave. PMB launched a thorough investigation, which led to him having to issue an official apology to me. It seems PMB has received a slew of complaints about this individual," Sammy eagerly leaned in, filling Kian in on every detail, her voice animated.

"What in the world? What a brazenly misogynistic jerk! You're absolutely hilarious when you're drunk. You should have shot back, 'And your wife's been eyeing your dinner!' Next thing you know, he'll be telling me not to embrace my identity—what an utter fool! To comment on your personal life in your own space is downright outrageous; who does he think he is? He would never dare say that to a man; he'd probably get his lights knocked out! We should swing by his house and offer him a masterclass in how to fuck his wife!" Kian erupted into laughter once more, the sound buoyant and infectious.

Sammy couldn't help but join in, a warm, rich laugh escaping her lips, fully aware that they were destined to get along like a house on fire.

"What do you think of the concierge?" he asked, curious.

Sammy's expression revealed her disdain, a mix of disbelief and frustration.

"Mark is decent, but the rest? They're lazy, misogynistic, nosy, and downright rude. It's a mystery how they've managed to keep their contract here. One of them actually had the audacity to say something to a guy I was casually seeing.

'Keep a leash on that, mate,' he said. I was utterly stunned," she recounted, her eyes wide.

Kian's eyebrows shot up in shock. "What the absolute fuck! That's incredibly rude; he ought to be fired! Which one is it? The older guy with the glasses, Stan?" he asked, a mix of anger and disbelief in his voice.

"Yes, indeed, the very same person. He even had the audacity to share details about another resident's relationship status—a close friend of mine—along with intimate snippets of his daily activities here, showing a complete and utter disregard for his privacy. If they're spreading gossip about the personal lives of residents, they have no place here. We're shelling out a hefty sum for concierge services, and this kind of disrespectful behaviour is downright unacceptable!" Sammy exclaimed passionately, her frustration bubbling to the surface like a simmering pot ready to boil over.

Kian shook his head in disbelief, a wry smile creeping across his face. "Stan is absolutely hopeless. My aunt and I can't help but chuckle whenever he's around. He struggles just to call a taxi, for crying out loud! Honestly, where do they find these incompetent people?" he complained, rolling his eyes in frustration.

"Then there's Stewart, that cantankerous old man, who is so incredibly inappropriate. Just the other day, he approached me and invited me to join him for coffee. That's sexual harassment, then he started making dubious comments about my figure and then launched into a tirade about Mitch, who lives in our building. He shared all sorts of unflattering gossip about Mitch's personal life as if it were entertainment. And don't get me started on Dick! He's as sharp as a dull knife; I can barely make sense of what he says. I once asked him to speak to the tenants in the penthouse above me because they were making a racket, dragging furniture across their floors in the middle of the night. But of course, he got it all wrong and complained to the neighbours next door instead. It's infuriating! He doesn't have a clue about the layout of the apartments because he spends all day sitting on his ample behind. Honestly, if there were ever a fire in this building, we'd be in serious trouble!" Sammy exclaimed, rolling her eyes in exasperation.

"Yes, Dick is thick. Oh bejesus, that rhymes—see what I did there?" Kian giggled.

"Thick Dick thick Dick, he ain't so quick, cos he's so thick!
Stew Stew in the eeigit crew, he's a dopey fecker too!
Stan Stan the dirty old man will make you retch cos he's a pervy letch
Misogynist Mike & his fat, ugly wife
Should keep their big noses out of our life"

"I should be a poet, Sammy, I really should," Kian laughed

"That's brilliant Kian." Sammy was howling with laughter.

I believe they forget that we pay for their services, making them accountable to us. The company seems to operate under the belief that we are accountable to them instead. They are very unproductive, and Stan complains whenever asked to help. He consistently criticises the residents and grumbles about PMB. They should install CCTV in that office, which would help stop the issues. If I were their boss, I would fire the team. I have never encountered a more unprofessional group in my life. It is even more alarming that they are violating GDPR by spreading rumours. I do not want my business discussed around the apartments, and I have a right to privacy; we all do," Sammy looked angry.

"Ah, well, Sammy, just do as I do and ignore the feckin' eeigit's!"

The rest of the evening was spent joyfully drinking on the deck, dancing, and laughing. She felt grateful for the new friend she had made.

"Have you seen the old, overweight woman who limps around the car park? She has gray hair and wears glasses; she is quite peculiar," Kian suddenly asked her mid-dance.

"Oh yes, I know who you mean," Sammy knew exactly who he meant.

"What a miserable cow! She stopped me near the lift a few days ago. I would rather chew glass than talk to her again. What is her name? Debbie? Debbie Downer?"

Sammy nearly spat her wine out as she laughed. He had described the woman perfectly; she was a miserable woman whom Sammy also tried to avoid.

"She needs to get a feckin' job and not wander the complex looking for people to spill her miserable life on. Is she married? I feel sorry for her husband if she is, fancy coming back home to that miserable heifer at night," Kian grimaced.

"I tend to avoid her as much as possible; I can't deal with miserable people because I'm just too positive. The job I do is dark—I listen to trauma and troubles all day—so I definitely don't want that negativity in my personal life. Her other friend is similar; you may have seen her—a dark-haired woman in her fifties who is an alcoholic. They have asked me to be friends with them, but I declined. Women like that annoy me. They are wealthy yet ungrateful, with nothing to do all day but drink or complain about life. I believe in having an attitude of gratitude; life is so much better that way. Her partner approached me and said I had upset her by declining to be her friend. Can you believe that? It's like we're back in school," Sammy sighed.

"Yes, I know her too. She is an alcoholic, she is always drunk, and her partner looks like a pot-bellied dwarf. I bet they are swingers with Debbie Downer and her husband. I think I know who her husband is, he's that weasley looking puny man in glasses, he is so thin, Debbie Downer has probably cut his balls off and ate them, he must be a closet gay too, and she looks like a lezzer!" Kian laughed again and began to sing. "Sleazy Weasley & Debbie Down, if they catch ya they'll make yer frown!"

"You are obsessed with people's weight," Sammy laughed.

"Probably, I was the Weight Watchers prize winner in Cavan a few years back. I was a fat bastard, but I lost it all. Do you think fat people know they are fat?" Kian said, looking quizzical.

"I have no idea," Sammy responded.

Around eleven pm, Kian escorted her back to her apartment. They exchanged hugs and phone numbers and made plans for the following Sunday.

Sunday night would be their night for catching up, wining, dining, and relaxing.

A day or two later, she had a reason to visit the concierge office to collect her parcels, where Stew was sitting.

"I see you and Kian are getting friendly. You should be careful; he's a drunk, you know," he said, looking down his nose at her.

"Kian's personal life is none of your business. You shouldn't speak about the residents like that. I shudder to think of what you say about me," Sammy glared at him.

"I heard you were a man-eater," he replied.

Sammy left the office, feeling shocked and dismayed.

Her next encounter was with Dick.

"Can you buzz Kian's intercom for me and ask him to meet me in the car park?" she asked.

"He doesn't know how to use his intercom," came the reply.

You're lying, Sammy thought, followed by, *What a moron.*

Chapter 3

PTSD & Denial

After the terrorist attacks in London, there had
been several suicides and suicide attempts amongst
law enforcement officers and a worrying number of
officers with PTSD symptoms, which were evident
to the trauma-informed. Still, unfortunately, the
top brass were firmly in denial about it.

Cambridge University carried out a research
programme with serving officers and discovered
that 1 in 5 had PTSD or CPTSD. Over 18,000 officers
had responded to the research.

On 25th November, she got into her car, Miss
Scarlett, and drove to the large Asda supermarket
in town, located just off St Paul's roundabout. She
often visited the supermarket to pick up essentials,
and the 25th November was no exception. As she
drove on Kynverton Road, she travelled at 30 mph
on her way home.

As she drove, she noticed a black VW Golf waiting
at the T-junction with Vale Road to her left. The
driver appeared to be distracted, looking down

at his lap, likely at his phone. Vale Road was on a steep hill, and she knew the driver would need to rev his engine to make it up the junction. A sinking feeling hit her, and she realized he was about to pull out and collide with her. Instinctively, she honked the horn to warn him, but it was too late.

The Golf crashed into her car from the side, sending Miss Scarlett skidding across the road. There was a loud bang, followed by an eerie silence. For a moment, she thought the car might be on fire as smoke filled the interior. Then she realised the airbag had deployed. Pain shot through the right side of her head, shoulder, elbow, hip, knee, and ankle.

"Are you okay? I'm an off-duty police officer. I witnessed what happened; he abruptly pulled out in to you. My name is Ryan."

"Yes, I'm okay, thanks, Ryan. I'm a retired West Midlands police officer, and you know what they say: there's never a cop around when you need one, right?" She managed a grin, but pain and worry about Miss Scarlett's condition were evident on her face.

"We should check on the driver of the VW," Ryan suggested. The VW driver was uninjured and accepted responsibility; they exchanged details, and both vehicles were drivable. She drove the mile home and parked the car.

She dialed Kian.

"I've been in a crash. Can you come to the car park?"

"Holy hell, Sammy! I'll be there in a jiffy!"

True to his word, he arrived with a look of concern and helped her up to her apartment. She took some painkillers and went to bed.

The next morning, she was extremely stiff; her neck, leg, and buttocks were sore, her knee hurt, and her right leg kept giving out. She took a taxi to the hospital.

While sitting in the waiting room, she texted her friend Chris in the US. He was about to retire in just a couple of months after 35 years of service.

"Hey, look what happened!" She added a picture of the damaged Miss Scarlett.

"Holy cow! Are you okay? You could have been killed!"

"Yes, I'm just at the emergency room getting checked out; I am a bit sore."

They exchanged texts on and off for four hours while she waited to be seen. The good news was that nothing was broken, so she returned home to handle her administrative tasks. She called her insurance company, who arranged to have the car picked up and provided her with a hire car. A few days later, she received the unfortunate news that Miss Scarlett would be sent to the car graveyard; she was deemed a total loss.

Sammy was frustrated; she needed to attend a conference in London and had to find a replacement car quickly. Fortunately, she located a silver Alfa Romeo nearby and purchased it. The insurance company had promptly processed her claim and had submitted a liability claim against the driver of the Volkswagen.

Sitting on Kian's deck later on that day, they named the new ride "Miss Silver". She was not the same as Miss Scarlett, but she was okay.

On Friday, 13th December, Sammy was invited to a conference on PTSD at King's College London, where several renowned keynote speakers were present. She drove to the conference with the intention of staying overnight at a hotel, but ultimately decided to drive back home instead. Although it was December, the weather was fine, although quite dark by the time the conference concluded. However, she wanted to get accustomed to driving Miss Silver.

Chris, in the US, called her while on his way home to check in on her. She used hands-free technology in her car.

"Hey, how did it go? Are you at your hotel?" Chris asked.

"It was informative and clear; everyone recognises the problem, but aligning all 43 forces is challenging."

"I know exactly what you are saying, Samantha, we have the same trouble here in the US, and we have a hell of a lot more forces or departments than you guys over the pond. We all need to get our ducks in a row," Chris responded.

"I decided to drive home, the weather isn't too bad today, it is getting cold though," Sammy said.

"My friend, you should see the winters over on the Eastern Seaboard. We experience Nor'easters that can cause significant havoc. Be careful on the drive home, and let me know you are safe. Text me when you get home," Chris sounded concerned.

"Ok, my friend, I will," she promised.

She drove home safely and gave Paws a hug on her return, and her favourite Lik-e-lix treat.

"Home safe," she texted Chris as she ran a bath.

Within seconds, her phone rang.

"Hey, how are you feeling? How's your injuries?" he enquired.

"Hi, I am still sore, my leg keeps giving way and I have a pain in my butt," she replied.

Chris burst out laughing, quipping, "Sorry I was just asking about ya didn't mean to be a pain in yer butt!"

Sammy laughed back, he was as quick-witted as she was, and they shared the same sense of humour.

"I have to go for physical therapy to sort my back out, I have 6 sessions booked. I think they are doing a mixture of massage and needling, hope the needling doesn't hurt, it's a type of acupuncture."

"What! It's only a couple of pricks in yer butt Samantha, you never had a prick in your butt before?" Chris burst out laughing.

"I may have, that's for me to know and you to find out," she laughed back.

"You should be fine. Can you bend over and touch your toes?" He was still laughing.

"Just about," she laughed back.

"Good, then you will be fine. I love you, Sam. Get some rest, and I will speak with you tomorrow."

"I love you, too, Chris."

Law enforcement officers often express their love for one another. This behaviour stems from their awareness of how precious life is and how quickly it can be taken away. Many people regret not sharing their feelings with loved ones or not having the chance to say goodbye.

Sammy woke up early and cuddled up to Paws for a few minutes, then their morning routine started. She put the kettle on as Paws followed her into the kitchen. Sammy got out her favourite cat treat, Like-lix, a type of yoghurt and gave it to her in her dish on the kitchen floor. She made a cup of tea with one sugar and skimmed milk and looked across the bay. The view from her kitchen was breathtaking, nothing but the pier and a vast expanse of the ocean in sight.

She took her hairband out and went to the bathroom, where Paws jumped in the bath, waiting for her to throw the hairband in. The shape of the bath meant Paws could chase it round and around without losing it under the furniture. Sammy was bemused. There were hundreds of cat toys on the market, but a simple hairband would bring hours of ample fun.

The second cup of tea started to wake her up; she always had 2 in the morning, one for each eye. She then began to focus on the day.

As a counsellor, she was required to complete 30 hours of Continuing Professional Development (CPD) each year. For the past year, she had been working on the keynote presentation for SCO19 and was considering getting it accredited for future use.

She sat at her desk and looked up accreditation bodies on the internet. The Continuing Professional Development Standards Office (CPDSO) in London came up, and she read with interest what it would entail. It would cost to get her course accreditation, but she could get five courses accredited for the same fee. After a phone call to their sales department and an explanatory conversation, she got to work on her Keynote and began to turn it into a training course.

The cost of accreditation for one year was approximately £1,500; however, obtaining CPD Accreditation would lend the course credibility. She had the time to give it some serious thought and design; it was coming up to Christmas, and work was quiet. Planning to design a few slides a day, she got to work on developing.

PTSD Awareness for Law Enforcement Officers & First Responders.

Anna's name popped up on her iPhone with a text that read, "Are you coming for Christmas dinner?"

"Of course, my lovely! I will be there by 1pm," Sammy texted back.

Little did she know that this would be the last time she would attend Christmas dinner for several years.

"I feel awful. I think I have the flu," Sammy texted.

"There's a lot of it going around; the kids all have it," Anna replied.

"Send them my love. See you soon. Love you loads," Sammy responded.

Anna sent back a smiley heart emoji, which always made her smile.

Christmas Day at Anna's was always excellent; the food was delicious, and Sammy loved Anna and her three children, Mia, Ewan, and Alfie. She had watched them grow up over the years into lovely teenagers, respectful, polite and considerate.

Anna's mother, Josephine, was a real lady too. She had married a naval officer and had a great life, living in different places across the globe, and she had many stories to tell.

Sammy was looking forward to their traditional Christmas gathering. Her thoughts momentarily deviated to presents for the kids, but then she returned to the task at hand.

An hour later, her iPhone pinged again.

"Can you bring me to the shop?" Kian added a smiley heart emoji.

"Sure, meet me at Miss Silver in 5."

Sammy was grateful for the distraction and pulled herself away from her desk; her backside was stiff, and her knee felt weak. The physical therapy was helping, and the therapist had told her that time would help as well.

Kian met her with a big grin in the underground car park at Miss Silver.

"Hello, what are you up to today?" he asked.

"Working on my training course, I am glad you texted. I was going stiff in the chair," Sammy replied.

"Shall we go to Home Bargains? I have to get some Christmas stuff," he asked her.

"Perfect, me too," she responded.

The drive along the Overcliff was stunning; the coast road was usually full of dogs and their owners, cyclists, and walkers. The ocean was always rolling in, and during the winter months, the white horses were wild.

"When are you going back to Cavan?" Sammy questioned.

My flight is booked for the 20th, can't wait to see the family, are you going to Anna Banana's ?" he asked back.

"Of course, hope the weather stays mild, the drive back can be treacherous on those lanes out by her place," Sammy said, her eyes widening.

"You sound like you have a cold, Sammy," Kian stated.

"Yeah, I do feel a bit rough, it's the time of year, I guess, Ki Ki," Sammy said, pulling into Barrack Lane.

Neither of them knew what was coming as they drove along the coast road; neither of them knew what the future was going to bring them both, nor did they know that COVID-19 was about to hit.

Chapter 4

Phoenix Heroes
CIC Veterans
PTSD Support

Via LinkedIn, Sammy was connected with Sue
Stockton, the founder of Phoenix Heroes CIC, and
her husband, Gary Stockton, a retired Warrant
Officer 1st Class who had served 22 years in the
British Army. Phoenix Heroes CIC Veteran PTSD
Support were based in Colchester in Essex and was
just getting off the ground.

Gary asked Sammy if she was interested in being
their Clinical Lead, as they had an interest in
supporting Armed Forces Veterans who had
been diagnosed with PTSD. Sammy jumped at
the chance; she felt that the military was her
family, and having served herself, she knew
the organisation well, including its structure,
communication methods, banter, and humour. Gary
and Sammy had a lengthy phone conversation, and
a service agreement was drawn up and signed by
both parties.

After considering the future, Sammy decided to write courses for Veterans on PTSD Awareness & Suicide Awareness, as figures in the US suggested that 22 Veterans a day were taking their own lives, and the prevalence of PTSD was colossal. There was little bona fide statistical data available in the U.K.

She then decided to write a further course on Suicide Awareness for Law Enforcement Officers & First Responders. That was now four courses to create; she got busy on her Mac. Over the next month, she made her courses and submitted them to the CPDSO (Continuing Professional Development Standards Office). She was on tenterhooks for the next 30 days waiting for their response. It had been bloody hard work, and she had put her heart and soul into them.

In early February 2020, Gary from Phoenix called her, his voice full of concern.

"I've got a Para in a right state, he is suicidal. Sam, can you help him?"

"Of course, text me his contact details," Sammy stated.

"I haven't got the funding for it yet, mate, but I will get it, I promise," he explained.

"Not a problem, I will do it buckshee," she replied.

"Oh, thank God, you are a good girl. I will send his contact details to you now," Gary said with his voice full of concern.

True to his word, the contact details pinged on her iPhone, and she contacted the client immediately.

The veteran signed her contract, and an appointment was made for the following day. Sammy provided 12 sessions for him over the next 3 months.

The Parachute Regiment is the airborne infantry regiment of the British Army, renowned as Britain's elite airborne infantry. It plays a crucial role in the UK's rapid response force and the Special Forces Support Group.

Paratroopers are trained for diverse missions, ranging from pre-emption and prevention to high-intensity combat. The Regiment specialises in deploying by parachute or through air assault into combat zones.

As part of the rapid response force, the 16 Air Assault Brigade Combat Team, and the Special Forces Support Group, paratroopers are prepared to deploy anywhere in the world. They are equipped for various operations, including high-intensity combat, counterinsurgency missions, and humanitarian assistance.

Paratroopers undergo rigorous training, which includes parachute jumping and combat skills. The Regiment was established during World War II as shock troops. They provide infantry support to Britain's rapid deployment force and specialised infantry assistance to the Special Forces. The 1 Battalion is permanently under the command of the Director of Special Forces, serving within the Special Forces Support Group.

The key values of the Parachute Regiment are professionalism, resilience, discipline, versatility, courage, and self-reliance.

Kian texted her early one Sunday morning in February.

"Sammy, I feel ill, can you come over?"

She went immediately and saw that his door was open.

On entering, she shouted.

"Kian, it's me. Where are you?"

"I am in bed," he replied with a weak, pained voice.

She went into his bedroom and saw him lying there looking deathly pale, a sick bowl full of green vomit on his lap.

She administered first aid to the best of her capability and then called an ambulance. Shortly after, two paramedics knocked on the door and went to assess him. After a thorough assessment, they told him he was to be admitted to the hospital. Kian looked terrified as they put him in a wheelchair and into the lift.

"I'll lock up Kian and get you some personal belongings and come down later, don't worry, you will be ok, you are going to the safest place you could go to," Sammy reassured him.

"Will you call Aunty and my mother, please, and let them know?" he said as his voice broke and he burst into tears.

"Sure, no problem, see you later, love you," Sammy said as she kissed him on the cheek.

She was concerned about her friend and went about packing him some underwear, a change of clothes and toiletries in his overnight bag. She then, as requested, called his aunt.

"Hello, this is Sammy. We met recently. I am Kian's friend. I need to tell you he has just been taken to Bournemouth Hospital, he is unwell."

"Bejesus, what is wrong with him?" Aunty asked in a voice full of concern.

"I have no idea, but his pulse was weak, he looked deathly pale, and he had been vomiting a lot. He asked me to go over, and after seeing him, I called an ambulance," Sammy told her.

"Oh, thank you so much, I will call him right now," she replied, sounding worried.

"Please, can you inform his mother, your sister? I don't know her number," Sammy stated.

"Of course, thank you, bye, Samantha," She hung up.

Sammy was concerned and attended the hospital later that evening. Kian was wired up in a private room, looking very ill.

"Do they know what is wrong with you yet?" she asked tentatively.

"No, they're going to do more tests tomorrow, but I have to stay in. Thanks for contacting Aunty, she has called and so has Mother," he said with gratitude.

"Are they going to fly over?" Sammy asked as she pulled up a chair at his bedside.

"Not sure yet, I will have to keep them updated," he said rolling his eyes, then added, "I am dying for a fag and a Jamesons."

Sammy visited every other day, and ten days later, Kian was finally released from the hospital. He remained unsure of what was wrong with him, or as Sammy suspected, he did not want that information to be revealed. When she picked him up, Sammy could see the relief on his face. They drove home in silence.

"There you go, home sweet home, I will catch you tomorrow," she smiled at him as she put the handbrake on.

He arrived at her door the next day with a massive bunch of flowers and a box of chocolates. Giving her a big hug, he said.

"You saved my life, thank you so much!"

"Have you seen what's on TV about this COVID-19 yet?" She looked serious.

"No, what?" he asked.

"Looks like some sort of viral epidemic, like SARS or Ebola, pretty scary, they've found cases in the UK," she informed him.

"What the fuck—that's scary!" Kian looked shocked.

"It is a worry, thank God you are out of the hospital," Sammy said, looking perplexed.

"How have you been? How's work?" he asked.

"Got a job with Phoenix Heroes as a counsellor, took on my first client. Yay!" Sammy said with a smile.

"Oh, hello, soldier!!!" Kian quipped.

Sammy thought he was hilarious and happy to have him home.

On 14th February, she received a Valentine's card from an admirer, which both surprised her and made her smile. It had been a long time since she had had an admirer, let alone received a Valentine's card. She texted him to express her gratitude, telling him she was very flattered.

Kian came for coffee early in the morning as he did most days, a flat white before she gave him a lift to work.

"So did ye get any Valentine's cards?" he asked with a twinkle in his eye.

"I did indeed, unexpected to say the least, I've never met the guy in person, just online."

"Love-Bomber!!!" Kian giggled.

"He's cute and separated, but there are so many catfishers out there, only time will tell."

Chapter 5

2020 & The Pandemic

"Have you seen the news?" Sammy asked Kian.

"Is this really for real?" Kian replied, astonished.

"Looks like it," Sammy said, grimacing.

"Welcome to the apocalypse!" Kian responded.

"Are you still going to work?" she inquired.

"No, the restaurant is closed," Kian said sadly.

Sammy looked at her friend and sighed. "What a nightmare."

The lunchtime BBC news showcased Boris Johnson as he firmly addressed the nation.

"You must stay at home," he declared.

Sammy listened intently as he announced that the country was entering a lockdown.

"You must wear a mask," the Prime Minister insisted.

Without hesitation, Sammy grabbed her phone, opened the Amazon app, and ordered a box of masks and gloves.

"You must practice social distancing," he reinforced.

Holy shit, this was getting worse by the minute. She lived alone, so she couldn't rely on others to get her essentials.

23rd March 2020, will be forever etched in her memory.

Watching the pandemic take hold of the world was horrifying. She was glued to the news, not wanting to watch it, but compelled to. Her apartment complex was eerily quiet. She noticed with disgust that the concierge team, including the fire marshals and the cleaners, were not wearing masks.

She challenged Stan;

"Well, it's not the law, is it? I've had a letter from my GP telling me I am in the vulnerable category," he stated sarcastically.

"Stan, you shouldn't be here, this isn't about you, think of other people not just yourself. You are handling 169 apartments parcels and keys and putting the residents at risk," Sammy explained.

"Is your parcel a vibrator? My mate likes dirty sex!" Stan lecherously eyed her, touching his penis over his trousers.

"You are disgusting, put a mask on, I will be reporting you to the relevant authorities and PMB and recording everything you say in future," Sammy walked out of the concierge office thoroughly disgusted and right into a fire marshal.

"Where's your mask? You are touching the entrance gate, every door, handrail and lift button in this apartment complex," Sammy challenged her.

"I don't like them, they make my glasses steam up," was the selfish response she gave.

After returning to her apartment, she emailed PMB to file a formal complaint and also informed the police.

Gary from Phoenix called her.

"Hey mate, how're you? I've got a lead for you from G4S, he's the veteran's mentor at HMP Parc in Wales. He's interested in your courses. Are they all accredited now?" He asked.

"Yes, Boss, that's great news. I'll give him a call," she said gratefully.

"How are things with you with this lockdown?" Gary enquired.

"Weird. Our concierge, fire marshals and cleaners are negligent, none are wearing PPE (personal protective equipment), and they're handling 169 apartments here," Sammy replied angrily.

"That's disgusting, mate, have you reported them?" He said in agreement.

"Of course, Boss, I'm still waiting to hear back from PMB," Sammy sighed.

"I'm working on getting funding, but it's hard. I'll keep you posted. Good luck with Chance at HMP Parc," Gary said.

"Cheers, Boss," Sammy said as Chance's number pinged on her phone.

Later that evening, she was sitting at her desk in the office with the window open when the stench of cannabis violently assaulted her nostrils. It was coming from the flat below her, which had two tenants in, young Liverpudlian men in their twenties. It reeked to high heaven, and was making her retch. Knowing that the only professional concierge Mark was on duty, she dialled him on the intercom and asked him to come up. A few moments later, he presented at her door wearing a mask.

"Hello Samantha, everything ok?" he asked.

"No, the tenants underneath me are smoking cannabis, and it's stinking my apartment out," she said, pulling a face.

"I will speak to them," Mark frowned.

Sammy liked him; he had been the head doorman at a local bar for years and was a big unit standing at 6ft 4.

"Thank you, I'm trying to work, and my office now stinks," she said, shaking her head.

She knew he would follow through; he did what he said he would do, unlike the others who sat on their lazy arses, moaning.

On Thursday at 4pm, the music from the apartment below started, booming loudly. "They've lost it," Sammy thought.

People started acting oddly due to being locked down, and the pressure was starting to show. She moved to her bedroom to reduce the noise and watched a film.

At 4am on Friday, it was even louder, and the shouts from their balcony had woken her up.

She dialled the concierge on her intercom.

"You're up early," said Stewart, one of the directors of the concierge company.

"The apartment below has had their music blasting for twelve hours; they've got guests and are having a party. Can you come across, please, and speak with them."

A few minutes later, he appeared, and as he approached the entrance to the block, Sammy opened her Juliet balcony and looked down. A tall lad in his twenties was hanging off the balcony below, clearly drunk.

"Can you turn that music down? It's four in the morning, and it's been going on for twelve hours," Sammy asked, her voice laced with anger.

"Don't come out here all guns blazing!" he snarled at her.

"We are in lockdown, and you don't live here. Turn the music off and leave," Sammy said assertively.

Stewart looked up and said.

"Well, actually, you are making more noise than they are," his tone was patronising.

Sammy pulled her phone out and pressed record.

"If you were doing your job, Stewart, you would have heard the party, smelled the cannabis and seen that this guy is not the tenant; they're breaching lockdown regulations. Also, Stewart, why aren't you wearing a mask? I am calling the police."

With that, the guy on the balcony immediately stepped into the apartment, and the music was switched off. Stewart turned on his heel and walked off.

Idiots! Sammy thought.

She emailed PMB again to complain about the concierge. They were allegedly licensed by the SIA and should know how to handle situations. Sammy wondered if they possessed fake licenses, as their customer service skills were appalling.

Crawling back into her bed, she looked at Paws and groaned. "The world is full of idiots, Paws, selfish, self-serving idiots."

A response from the PMB Property Management arrived later that week. It was apathetic, stating that PMB wore their masks when attending the apartments, with no mention of the concierge's or fire marshal's behaviour.

Sammy started to dig. The concierge company had been set up by Dick. Then Dick & Stewart set up DFSB Ltd, which was the fire marshal company. Now it was making sense. Sammy wondered if any of them had any qualifications, or indeed if they were registered CCTV operators. She then laughed as she gave the letters DFSB the meaning, Dopey Feckin' Stupid Bastards Ltd.

Like a dog with a bone, she emailed PMB and DFSB Ltd asking for a copy of their complaints procedures, the SIA licenses for CCTV, and clarification of their roles and responsibilities. However, there was no response.

It was strange outside. Every couple of days, she went to the shop for supplies, wearing both a mask and gloves. On her way, she spotted a car pull into the disabled bay just outside her apartment block in the public car park. A guy brazenly stepped out, pulled out a surfboard, and began preparing to go surfing. She couldn't help but take on the challenge.

"What are you doing? We are in lockdown," she called out.

"I work for the police; I can surf here," he replied.

"Really? Can you park in a disabled bay without being disabled? What's your collar number and which force do you belong to?"

He looked at the ground, avoiding her gaze.

"Right, I'm reporting you. You're putting lives at risk," Sammy said, snapping a photo of him and his car's registration number.

Arriving at the shop, a man wearing "Security" on the back of his jacket pulled onto the double yellow lines, got out of his van without any personal protective equipment (PPE), and walked in before her.

"Where's your mask?"

"In the van," he replied sheepishly.

"Where's your SIA licence? Who do you work for?"

Sammy shot him her best death stare. She hadn't earned the nickname "Lemon Sucker" for nothing; she had perfected her "Resting Bitch Face," Pulling out her iPhone, she snapped a photo of him and his van.

"I hope they fire you, you should know better, you are putting lives at risk," she told him.

After picking up her groceries, she headed back to her apartment. On her way, she ran into the other female fire marshal. There were rumors that the marshal was in a relationship with Stewart, who was at least 30 years older than her—ick! Additionally, the marshal was not wearing a mask.

Oh quelle surprise! she thought to herself, then in with the challenge.

"Where's your mask?" She asked.

"Oh, er, er, I normally wear one," she stammered.

"No, you don't, I've been watching you since lockdown started, get a mask on! You are going in and out of all the apartment blocks, opening all the entrance doors, using the lifts and touching the stair rails, do you not understand you are putting the residents at risk?"

Silence.

"Disgusting behaviour," Sammy glared at her.

"I will be reporting you all to the police, I hope you get fined."

•Between 1 March and 30 April 2020, there were 33,841 deaths caused by COVID-19 in the UK.
•171,253 people had tested positive, and 15,043 were hospitalised.
The NHS were facing their worst nightmare. Source - Office for National Statistics.

Chapter 6

Madness In May

Sammy was bored; she only had one client and was so upset that, due to lockdown, no one could attend her course. HMP Parc was locked down, and its budget was impacted by the need to implement safety measures.

Phoenix Heroes were struggling to get funding.

The world was getting more bleak by the day. Compelled to watch the news morning, lunchtime and evening, she sat horrified on her own. Watching the impact on other countries and the impact on the NHS on the news compounded the fear and sadness she felt. This was scary, probably the most terrifying thing she had personally encountered. She had no control, and it was that lack of control that scared her the most.

Struggling to put her time to good use, she became depressed and lethargic. Texts from Kian and Anna became less and less, and the fear in people's eyes was striking. Her visits to the shops became sporadic, and she was acutely aware that she was falling into depression, or possibly PTSD, a pandemic was in the criteria in the Diagnostic & Statistical Manual (DSM-5).

Deciding to write another book, she contacted her publisher in Florida and discussed the details of "Suicidal Mate," Finally, she had a distraction.

The news abounded with images of the effects of COVID-19, and not surprisingly, the incidents of domestic violence were increasing. Shelves housing essentials like water, milk and toilet paper in the supermarket were emptying at an alarming rate, and people were starting to turn on each other. The Pandemic was divisive.

Writing was an adaptive coping mechanism for her; she began to focus and write.

Chapter 7

Suicidal Ideation

A colleague sent a message to her phone:

"I'm having a really bad day."

She replied right away, "I understand. I'm having a tough day too."

"Do you think God will forgive me for what I have done?" he pressed.

"Absolutely, but you need to call me," Sammy insisted.

"I don't think life is worth living anymore," he confessed.

"You need to call me right now!" she demanded.

She waited and waited, feeling her heart rate increase and her senses heighten. She loved this guy; they were firm friends, and he served in law enforcement. Hours passed, and there was no response. She called his phone; it went straight to voicemail. She had a terrible night, not able to sleep, worried about her colleague. She texted the following morning.

"Please call me."

No response.

She checked his social media for signs of life, but there was nothing posted for days, which was unusual as his norm was to post daily. They were also usually in daily contact, so not hearing from him raised more red flags. She called his phone again; it went straight to voicemail. She decided to give him another 24 hours to get in touch, then she was going to call the police to request a safe & well check.

A further 24 hours passed, no social media, no texts, no callback. She contacted his local police and requested a safe and well check, citing the texts he had sent. They did not call her back. She guessed they would be pretty busy.

Needing to clear her mind, she got in Miss Silver and went for a long drive over to Blandford, driving past Anna's house and then Josephine's house, she sent them her love and wished them all the best in her mind. She put her favourite playlist on and drove for hours, triggering fond memories of her time in Bournemouth with friends.

As a behavioural therapist, she knew that thoughts affect feelings, which in turn affect behaviour.

Still, she was struggling not to be overwhelmed by thinking that her colleague had taken his life.

Kian texted her:

"Sammy, this is awful. Can I come over?"

"No, Kian. We are in lockdown, so you can't come over."

Sammy understood that maintaining her distance was essential for her focus; he was clearly struggling.

"I feel like throwing myself off the balcony," he texted.

"Listen to me, Ki Ki. Hang in there. You need to find something to distract yourself; it's important," she replied firmly.

"I want to go home to Ireland, and I can't," Kian responded.

"You need to be patient. Everything will be okay. Just trust the process," Sammy asserted.

The day passed with her focusing on her book and sleeping on and off.

Bright and early the following morning, on her way to Miss Silver, she encountered "Debbie Downer" in the car park. "Oh no!" she thought, trying to avoid her.

"Oh, Sam!" Debbie exclaimed, bursting into tears.

"My husband has been laid off, and the concierge is not paying attention to COVID-19 regulations. They are allowing second homeowners to come down to their apartments, and people are having parties and inviting guests. I am incredibly angry, my leg hurts, and we're in financial trouble with loans and a mortgage. I feel overwhelmed and desperate. Please help me!"

Debbie Downer stood like a little girl in the car park, crying.

"I'm sorry to hear that. We are all affected. I have to go now. Bye," Sammy got in her car and drove off.

Debbie Downer shot her a filthy look, sniffed in disgust and limped off.

"Go away, you toxic woman," Sammy thought to herself.

She knew that to survive this madness, she would have to distance herself. She had financial difficulties too; the last three months had brought zero income in, but she still had bills to pay.

Sammy knew it would be unethical to counsel Kian or Debbie Downer; she felt for Kian, but the ethical framework forbids a counsellor to counsel anyone with whom they are in a relationship, be that a friend, neighbour or family member.

The world was going mad, and there was nothing she could do about it but protect herself.

She texted Anna,

"Hope you are ok, I see the schools have closed, has the University closed too?"

Anna was attending University, doing a Law Degree.

"Yes, we are all at home," Anna texted back.

"How are you coping?" Sammy replied.

"The kids love it, I am studying from home for University, I think they are planning to do everything online," Anna answered.

"Good luck, give my love to the kids and mother," Sammy added the smiley heart emoji.

May dragged on endlessly. She watched her neighbours repeatedly break the restrictions, meeting for drinks on the terrace and gathering on the beach. She felt dismayed.

The more the public ignored the law and guidelines from the government, the more people would get infected and die, and the longer it would take to get the virus under control.

She noticed how long her hair was getting; she hadn't had it cut for two months, and her fringe was way down her face. She ordered some hair scissors online, then some dye. It would give her something to do.

She watched many box sets on TV, with Chicago PD and Spooks as two of her favourites, and grew increasingly lethargic as the days went by.

The death count was getting higher and higher, and the number of infections and admissions to the hospital was alarming. She tested herself with the available kits twice a week but never once contracted the virus.

A book available on Amazon caught her eye,

"Treating Police Stress: The Work and Words of Peer Counsellors" by John H Madonna, JR. & Richard E Kelly.

She ordered it and looked forward to reading it.

The concierge office was still open, which seemed odd, as they were not essential workers; she texted them.

"Please deliver any parcels I receive."

She would quarantine them herself before opening them and wear gloves as an additional safety measure. Knowing that only Mark was complying with the law, she no longer wanted to go to the concierge office or anywhere near the fire marshals.

The response came back.

"You will have to collect from the office. Do not come in; we will hand your parcels to you through the window."

Writing her book kept her busy and distracted; she couldn't see any clients face-to-face due to lockdown, and she did not, at that stage, have the means to conduct online video counselling.

The BACP were developing a training course so that she could become proficient in online counselling, but that meant she would have to buy the software to do it. Zoom seemed the most practical option, so she purchased a yearly package and hoped for the best. She undertook the training in online counselling and gained a certificate. The government also classified her as an essential worker.

Time dragged by so slowly, she knew some people were happy to be off and furloughed, but she wasn't; having no income for three months was draining her savings, and she was restless and bored.

On the phone, a former colleague with 30 years' service concurred with her on how DFSB Ltd showed blatant disregard for the residents' safety, amongst other glaring breaches of law and professional conduct.

"People are selfish, Sammy, stupid and self-serving, and concerning your concierge service, they are hardly going to be bright, are they, if you pay peanuts, you get monkeys."

Walking into the underground car park the following morning, she ran into another resident who was a sexual harasser; he was a nightmare. He had no understanding of personal space or boundaries. Every time they interacted, he would touch her, a little touch on the shoulder, the hip or the hand. She hated that and would step backwards to increase the space between them. He would step forward and get closer. "The new social distancing rule must be killing him," she mused.

Previously, he had knocked at her door to inform her that a bike had been stolen from the bike store. What on earth would she want to know that for? It wasn't her job to maintain security; it was the concierge's remit. He had called her intercom and disturbed her when she had guests, with nothing more to say than "One of the goats died," Again, why on earth would she be interested in that? Her response was "Well, curry it and serve with rice & pea," Jeez, what a pain in the arse.

She tried to get to her car quickly, but to no avail, he ran at her.

"Stop! We are socially distancing, and where is your mask?" Sammy challenged him, wishing he would go away.

"There is no such thing as COVID-19; this is a government plot to get us all injected with tracking serum and kill off the weak and the old," he told her.

She looked at him, glad that she had a mask on, as he could not see her jaw drop.

"Have a good day," she shook her head at him, got in her car, and drove away.

Chapter 8

Taking the Knee

George Perry Floyd Jr. was an African American man whose death during an arrest on May 25, 2020, ignited a powerful movement against police brutality and systemic racism. The chain of events began when a store clerk raised concerns about a suspected counterfeit twenty-dollar bill. This led to the involvement of four police officers, including Derek Chauvin, who infamously knelt on Floyd's neck and back for over nine minutes, resulting in Floyd's death. This incident became a catalyst for widespread protests demanding justice and accountability for police violence, particularly towards the Black community.

Floyd had a troubled past, with eight convictions between 1997 and 2005, and he served four years in prison after accepting a plea deal for an aggravated robbery during a home invasion. In 2014, he relocated to the Minneapolis area, settling in St. Louis Park, where he worked hard as a truck driver and bouncer. Unfortunately, in 2020, the COVID-19 pandemic led to the loss of both of his jobs.

The George Floyd protests erupted, characterised by demonstrations, riots, and a resolute stand against police brutality, starting in Minneapolis on May 26, 2020. This surge of civil unrest was directly fuelled by Floyd's death and rapidly spread across the nation and globally. The movement mobilised within hours, driven by impactful bystander videos and the immediacy of social media.

Protests began at the intersection of East 38 Street and Chicago Avenue in Minneapolis, where Floyd was arrested and ultimately died. These protests gained momentum, expanding to over 2,000 cities and towns in more than 60 countries, all rallying behind the Black Lives Matter (BLM) movement.

In many cities, demonstrations escalated into significant confrontations, including riots and looting, as tensions flared between protesters and law enforcement. The police were deployed to manage these situations with necessary measures. By early June 2020, curfews were enforced in at least 200 U.S. cities, and over 30 states, along with Washington, D.C., mobilised more than 96,000 service members from the National Guard, State Guard, 82nd Airborne Division, and 3rd Infantry Regiment. This represented one of the largest peacetime military mobilisations in U.S. history, necessitated by the gravity of the situation compounded with ongoing pandemic responses.

By late June 2020, the United States faced
overwhelming challenges, with over 14,000
people arrested and 19 lives lost amid the unrest.
From May 26 to June 8, the nation experienced
rampant arson, vandalism, and looting, leading to
an astonishing $12 billion in insured damages—
marking the highest toll from civil disorder in
U.S. history and surpassing the devastating
impact of the 1992 Los Angeles riots. This moment
underscored the urgent need for systemic reform
and accountability within law enforcement.

The protests triggered a wave of demonstrations
across the UK, and Sammy watched the riots on TV
with anger and disappointment. Riots and rallies
during a lockdown are completely irresponsible.
What were these people thinking? They need to
recognise the bigger picture: we are in the midst of
a global pandemic that has already cost countless
lives and damaged the economy. It is utterly foolish
to go out and inflict millions of pounds worth
of damage on their own communities. Are they
mentally unstable? It seems they are just looking
for an outlet for their fear, anger, and frustration.
Who do they expect will pay to fix the destruction
they've caused? They should be held accountable
for their actions—either by cleaning up their mess
or facing the consequences of their choices.

Having witnessed the Aston Riots in Birmingham
in 1985, she couldn't help but shudder at how they
began. The unrest was ignited by a Black man

who protested his arrest for smoking cannabis, an illegal substance in the UK. From her perspective, the decision of other countries to legalise cannabis is misguided. The potential for addiction can lead to severe consequences, including paranoia and schizophrenia, which cannot be ignored.

A study led by researchers at the Mental Health Services in the Capital Region of Denmark and the National Institute on Drug Abuse (NIDA) has found that young men with cannabis use disorder have an increased risk of developing schizophrenia. Published in *Psychological Medicine*, the study analysed health records data over a span of 50 years, representing more than 6 million people in Denmark. The researchers aimed to estimate the proportion of schizophrenia cases that could be attributed to cannabis use disorder at the population level.

Researchers have found strong evidence of a link between cannabis use disorder and schizophrenia in both men and women, with the association being particularly significant among young men. The study authors used statistical models to estimate that as many as 30% of schizophrenia cases in men aged 21-30 could have been prevented by addressing cannabis use disorder.

Both cannabis use disorder and schizophrenia are serious, yet treatable mental disorders that can profoundly impact people's lives. Individuals with cannabis use disorder are unable to stop using cannabis even when it leads to negative consequences. Schizophrenia is a severe mental illness that affects a person's thoughts, feelings, and behaviours. Those with schizophrenia may appear to have lost touch with reality, and its symptoms can hinder everyday activities.

The relationship between substance use disorders and mental illnesses poses a significant public health concern. Previous studies have indicated that rates of daily or near-daily cannabis use, cannabis use disorder, and new diagnoses of schizophrenia are higher among men than women. Early and frequent cannabis use is associated with an increased risk of developing schizophrenia.

Over the past few decades, the legalisation of cannabis has made it one of the most commonly used psychoactive substances worldwide, while decreasing public perception of its potential harms. This study contributes to the growing understanding that cannabis use carries risks that are not fixed over time and should be taken seriously.

The majority of law-abiding citizens in the UK are far more refined than the few who resort to rioting; they express their concerns through petitions rather than through violence or destruction. Most UK citizens understand right from wrong, are aware of the consequences of breaking the law, and support appropriate punishments. In fact, a large majority believe that some punishments are insufficient and advocate for longer sentences, increased prison capacity, and even the reintroduction of corporal punishment. Sammy was one of those who shared this view. Thankfully, cannabis remained a banned substance in the UK.

In the United States, the trend of fatal police shootings has been on the rise, with the rate among Black Americans significantly higher than that of any other ethnic group. Between 2015 and 2024, there were 6.1 fatal shootings per million of the Black population annually.

Sammy wondered why these statistics were so high. Was it due to a higher prevalence of drug addiction and mental illness among Black individuals? Did it stem from a larger number of Black individuals being confrontational towards law enforcement? Or perhaps it resulted from a greater level of police bias impacting behaviour? These questions warranted further examination.

The UK has historically faced challenges in recruiting Black and Asian police officers. Sammy was unaware of the answers to these issues and didn't find the gender disparity in policing bothersome; she felt comfortable in her role.

Having dated Black boys in her teens and having Black friends in school, she had worked with Black officers and could not understand racism; for her, an idiot was simply an idiot, regardless of race, gender, age, religion, or sexual orientation. She recognised that racial, ethnic, cultural, gender, and religious biases exist, as do preconceived beliefs and attitudes toward certain groups. Perhaps the notion of "police bias" contributed to some Black individuals' behaviours. No research had yet addressed this idea, but it should be explored further. The police often stand as a barrier between criminals and their lawlessness.

Sammy recalled a complaint that was lodged against her by a Black female officer in 1992. The issue originated from Sammy's straightforward question about whether the officer knew the lyrics to Snow's song *Informer*. The officer perceived this question as racist, but the complaint was clearly unfounded and ultimately dismissed.

Frustrated by the news and the foolishness of those around her, Sammy turned to LinkedIn and was pleasantly surprised to find a course available through FBI-LEEDA titled "Women in Policing," it was hosted by Mary O'Connor, BA, Terri Wilfong, (MS, M.S.M.), and Dr. Neil Moore, Ed.D.

The hour-long course was exactly what she needed. Numerous women police chiefs were in attendance, and it felt reassuring to be surrounded by educated individuals whom she believed would not engage in rioting or disregard lockdown laws afterward.

Chapter 9

42 Commando Royal Marines and Avon & Somerset Police

42 Commando is an essential component of the Royal Marines' Commando Force, specifically designated as part of the Maritime Operations Commando (MarOps Cdo). This elite unit specialises in conducting critical maritime security operations and providing training to allied forces across the globe. Since its establishment in August 1943, 42 Commando has built a reputation as a Very High Readiness (VHR) unit, distinguished by its robust capability to execute a wide range of special operations with a particular focus on maritime environments. The unit is strategically headquartered at Bickleigh Barracks, positioned near Plymouth in Devon, which facilitates efficient access to training areas and deployment opportunities.

The core mission of 42 Commando revolves around undertaking Maritime Security Operations (MSO), where they leverage their expertise in navigating complex maritime threats. The unit is recognised for its proficiency in high-threat maritime security measures, operational interdiction, and Joint Personnel Recovery (JPR), which involves the recovery of personnel in adversarial situations. Additionally, their skill set includes executing Maritime Interdiction Operations (MIOps), which are critical for safeguarding shipping lanes and combating unlawful maritime activities.

Operations conducted by 42 Commando encompass a diverse array of challenges, including maritime interdiction tasks aimed at disrupting illegal smuggling and trafficking activities, as well as counter-piracy initiatives designed to protect commercial vessels from piracy and maritime crime. They are also adept at coordinating pilot rescues in high-stakes scenarios, demonstrating their versatility and readiness to respond to emergencies at sea. Beyond these activities, 42 Commando plays a pivotal role in Support and Influence Operations (S&I), working to enhance security cooperation and build local partnerships through training and mentorship. This multifaceted approach underscores their commitment to maritime security and global stability.

42 Commando is not only a key player in critical military operations but also takes a prominent role in training allied forces abroad. Their training

programs are carefully designed to bolster the high-threat capabilities of these partnered units, ensuring readiness for a range of challenging scenarios. In addition to their training missions, they provide vital ship force protection teams, underscoring their commitment to maintaining security at sea. This elite unit is frequently deployed outside the United Kingdom, where they execute both operational missions and a variety of training exercises.

Recently, 42 Commando showcased their advanced skill set in a specialised warfare training exercise conducted in the Arctic. This intensive training was part of NATO's Steadfast Defender 24 exercise, where they prepared for a range of potential threats, including chemical, biological, radiological, and nuclear scenarios. The harsh and demanding environment of the Arctic served as an ideal backdrop for honing their capabilities, ensuring that they remain primed for any future contingencies.

Originally established in August 1943 from the remnants of the 1 Royal Marine Battalion, 42 Commando distinguished itself during World War II, particularly in the challenging terrains of India and Burma. Their valour was prominently displayed in the Battle of Kangaw in January 1945, where they engaged in fierce combat operations. Since the war, 42 Commando has continued to operate decisively across various global conflict zones, solidifying its reputation as a formidable force adept at navigating the complexities of modern military engagements. Their legacy is not just defined by their historical achievements, but also by their ongoing mission to adapt and excel in ever-evolving military landscapes.

Many armed forces veterans enlist in the military as a means of escaping the turmoil of dysfunctional families. In search of a new sense of belonging, they find camaraderie among fellow soldiers, often feeling as though they have joined a different family altogether. For many, this choice is also about seeking structure and discipline—elements that may have been sorely lacking in their chaotic home lives.

Dysfunctional families can resemble stormy seas filled with unpredictability and strife. They frequently suffer from addiction, violence, and various forms of abuse—psychological, physical, or sexual. In such turbulent environments, children may feel like castaways, grappling with feelings of being unloved and unwanted. They often carry a haunting belief that there is something fundamentally wrong with them, a profound weight that shadows their every step.

Sammy listened to his story with deep understanding and empathy. Although he maintained a stoic demeanour and spoke in a matter-of-fact tone, it was clear that his experiences weighed heavily on him. This way of communicating is often seen in those who have served in law enforcement and the military, as they've been trained to mask their emotions while still carrying the burdens of their past.

"I genuinely want to help you take back control of your life. I truly empathise with what you're saying, and I'm deeply sorry for all the pain you've endured. It's completely understandable that you've developed Complex PTSD (C-PTSD) from everything you've experienced. You've faced trauma in incredibly difficult environments and have suffered serious assaults. Just like a professional football player is likely to sustain an injury at some point due to the nature of their work, it's natural that you are feeling this way given what you've been through. Does that resonate with you?" she asked.

"Now that you put it that way, I understand," he replied, his voice softening.

"So, how does that connect to your deployments and service with the police? How many traumatic incidents have you experienced?" Sammy asked, her concern evident.

"Thousands," he said quietly, looking down.

"Would you say you might be at risk for developing C-PTSD?" she gently inquired.

"Yes, that makes sense," he agreed, a hint of relief in his tone.

"Congratulations, welcome to the club. I have it too, and so do thousands of other military and law enforcement veterans. It's something we've earned through our experiences, and it doesn't mean you're a coward or lazy. It's a normal response to what we go through," she responded, using familiar military language but with care.

"Oh, I thought of it as a weakness," he admitted, sounding vulnerable.

"You're not alone in feeling that way, but I want to assure you that it's not a weakness," Sammy said, her voice warm. "Think of it this way: PTSD is a moral brain injury caused by trauma. If you weren't affected by what you've been through, it would mean you're not human—and you are. Your diagnosis doesn't indicate that you're weak; it shows that you're human, feeling the weight of your experiences."

"Oh, thank you. I really appreciate your support. I feel a little better talking about this now. I've been seeing doctors and psychiatrists through the NHS, but it's been quite challenging for me. I often find it hard to understand what they're saying, and sometimes it feels like they're talking down to me. I don't feel like they truly understand what I'm going through. I'm not ready to share what happened in the theatre with them, but I feel more comfortable expressing it to you. It's frustrating that there's a lack of continuity in the NHS—it's a different person every time I seek help. I even had a counsellor who broke down in tears during a session and had to leave, which left me feeling more lost," he said, exasperated.

"Okay, I completely understand. I went through something similar when a male psychotherapist broke down in one of my sessions. It really threw me off, and I decided not to go back," she shared gently.

"I can relate. We dedicate ourselves to protecting others, but I don't think she could have handled what I've witnessed. It feels much more comfortable talking to you because you truly understand the reality I face," he said with a hint of sadness.

"I appreciate you sharing that. I'd like you to create a trauma timeline for me, listing all the significant traumas you've encountered. To support you through this process, I'll also send you a trigger diary, just in case any emotions come up. Does that sound good to you?" Sammy offered compassionately.

"That sounds like a solid plan, thank you!" he replied, feeling reassured.

"Ok, how do you feel about booking in for next week? We're looking at 12 weeks initially. How does that sound?" Sammy asked.

"I will, yes. Thank you, Sam; it really feels like you understand me," he said, letting out a deep sigh.

"I do, and it's because we've both walked similar paths. I also have to manage my C-PTSD," she shared, her voice reflecting her compassion.

Sammy immediately got to work, sending him a PDF on psychoeducation along with the two worksheets she had mentioned. She felt a warmth in her heart as she smiled to herself; finally, she had a paying client, and the fact that it was her brother brought a special sense of purpose to her day—a feeling that often resonates within military and law enforcement families.

As Sammy stepped into the warmth of June, the air was thick with the scent of blossoming flowers and the promise of summer. During her upcoming session with her client, the atmosphere shifted as he opened up about a deep, unsettling wound. He spoke of Floyd's death, a poignant reminder of the world's harsh realities, and how the chaos of the ensuing riots had unleashed a torrent of memories long buried in his mind. The tumult of those riots, filled with shouts and upheaval, reverberated through him, resurrecting feelings he thought he had left behind.

They reached a shared understanding about the unfortunate choices made by those involved in the subsequent riots, and they delved into a discussion about Chauvin's use of force. Her client opened up about several incidents he had encountered and shared his thoughts on what he deemed to be reasonable force. He acknowledged that this concept is often subjective and has never been clearly defined in the law.

After completing his trauma timeline, Sammy took a moment to read through it, noticing the many boxes he had checked.

"Which incident weighs on your heart the most?" she gently inquired.

"The girl who was trapped in her car and burned to death," he replied, his voice thick with emotion. "I can still smell it, hear her screams, and picture the driver who was drunk and at fault. I tried to pull her out; I even got burned in the process. My arms were on fire, and the smell of my singed hair still haunts me. I couldn't save her," as he spoke, a heavy silence settled between them, and the pain in his eyes was palpable. Sammy maintained the quiet, creating a safe space for him to share the weight of his feelings, fully aware of how difficult it can be to face such profound trauma.

"It was horrible," he said softly.

"How do you feel when you talk about it?" she gently asked, concerned for his emotional well-being.

"Not much, to be honest. I feel numb, and the medication I'm on leaves me pretty spaced out," he admitted, his vulnerability evident.

"How do these experiences affect you? What do you notice in your body?" Sammy asked with genuine curiosity, wanting to understand his psychosomatic symptoms.

"At night, I have terrible nightmares. I wake up screaming, drenched in sweat, and now I have to sleep in a separate bed from my wife. She's also ex-job," he shared, a hint of sadness in his voice.

"Does she understand what you're going through?" Sammy inquired, compassionately.

"She has been incredibly supportive, and my former colleagues have shown me a lot of understanding as well. I even had the opportunity to discuss my experiences in a documentary about violence towards police officers; it's called Critical Incident. I'm open about my struggle with C-PTSD," he shared.

"But have you come to terms with it and accepted that you're not the same person you once were?" Sammy gently asked.

"To some extent, I really miss my old self. I feel like I've lost my sense of purpose now that I am medically retired," he admitted, his voice reflecting a deep sadness and a sense of being lost.

"I need you to complete another assessment form called the PSS-I-5. This tool consists of 24 items and is designed as a semi-structured interview to evaluate PTSD symptoms experienced over the past month. The assessment is grounded in the diagnostic framework outlined in the DSM-5, which is the Diagnostic and Statistical Manual of Mental Disorders, Fifth Edition, published by the American Psychiatric Association. This manual serves as the authoritative guide for identifying and diagnosing various mental health disorders.

The assessment process starts with a criterion A trauma screen, which is crucial for identifying if a traumatic event has occurred. If an individual reports multiple trauma experiences, we will focus on identifying a primary or 'index' trauma for further evaluation. The questions that follow assess both the frequency and intensity of 20 specific PTSD symptoms defined by the DSM-5.

Additionally, there are four supplementary items included in this assessment that gauge the level of distress caused by these PTSD symptoms. They also explore how much these symptoms interfere with the individual's daily functioning. Lastly, we will examine the onset and duration of the symptoms to gain a comprehensive understanding of the individual's experience with PTSD."

She emailed him the document and talked him through the sample question.

Have you had unwanted distressing memories about the trauma?

0 = Not at all

1 = Once a week or less/a little

2 = 2 to 3 times a week/somewhat

3 = 4 to 5 times a week/very much

4 = 6 or more times a week/severe

The assessment took up the rest of their session.

"Do you want to talk about the medications I'm taking?" her client asked.

"Yes, that would really help me understand your situation better. If you could email me that information, I'd appreciate it. For your homework this week, I'd like you to write a goodbye letter to the girl in the car. Please don't hold back—share everything you're feeling, whether it's anger, sadness, pity, fear, disgust, or pain. This is a chance for you to find some closure. We can discuss what to do with the letter next week. How does that sound to you?" she asked gently.

"Okay, I will do it. Thanks," he replied, feeling a sense of agreement and understanding.

"If you feel any emotions, let them come, it's ok to feel, it's what makes us human, I know you were in The Royal Marines but you are still a human under the uniform and you have to learn that having emotions is not a sign of weakness, if you internalise your feelings you will become ill. The mind and the body are linked, your emotions will come out in ugly ways if you don't process them.

Aggression, alcoholism and recklessness to name a few. You may even feel suicidal, please let me know if you do and we can work through it. It is normal to feel suicidal when you have C-PTSD. I want us to make a verbal contact now that if you are feeling suicidal you will tell me, and you won't act on any ideation, ok?" she said.

"Yes, ok, I promise," he replied. "Ok brother we are now suicide contracted. I will speak with you next week, take care," she said.

"Thanks Sam, see you next week," he responded.

Sammy and her client have had 30 sessions to date.

Chapter Ten

The Long Hot Summer

The sun blazed fiercely overhead, casting shimmering heat waves over the empty beach, where the only sound was the distant crash of waves. Sammy was grappling with the new normal, her heart heavy as the death toll climbed steadily, an ominous shadow looming over the country. The NHS was stretched thin, trying desperately to manage the overwhelming surge of patients. In search of a creative outlet and a sense of control, she decided to transform her apartment with fresh paint. However, as she looked around at the quiet chaos, she realised her client work had come to a frustrating halt.

Just then, her phone buzzed with a message from Gary at Phoenix.

"Hey Sam, I've got a female client for you. She's married to a warrant officer. While she's not a veteran, she is battling PTSD," he said, his tone a mix of urgency and reassurance.

"That's fantastic! Send me her details, and I'll reach out to her today to schedule an appointment this week. Right now, I'm down to just one client, which feels so limiting. How are things going with you and Sue?" she responded, her voice upbeat in contrast to the heavy atmosphere.

"Yeah, all good, mate. But this pandemic feels like a nightmare. It's disheartening to see so many people flouting the rules while lives hang in the balance," he replied, a trace of sorrow creeping into his words.

"It's heartbreaking, isn't it? My neighbours are acting the same way. It makes my blood boil— such self-centred behaviour," Sammy replied, her frustration bubbling over.

"The silver lining is that schools are reopening now. That's a step in the right direction, but I wouldn't be surprised if many parents opt to keep their kids at home," he added, his voice reflecting a cautious hope mingled with concern.

Sammy thoughtfully remarked, "It's true; I really appreciate the two-metre rule. I've always felt uncomfortable with people in my personal space, and the shop where I get my essentials is usually nice and quiet."

When her iPhone buzzed with the client's details, Sammy reached out without hesitation.

"Hi, I'm Samantha from Phoenix Heroes. Gary has shared your number with me. Are you available for a chat right now?"

Suddenly, the client started to sob.

Sammy patiently waited in silence, allowing her space to breathe.

"Everything is wrong," her client finally managed to say, her voice trembling.

"Please, take your time. What's been weighing on your heart?" Sammy gently encouraged.

"The world feels crazy right now, and I feel lost—especially with everything going on with my husband," the client confessed.

For the next 50 minutes, Sammy listened intently as her client poured out her feelings and experiences.

Over the course of their 12 sessions together, they built a strong therapeutic alliance, which came to a close on 21st August 2020.

On 25th June 2020 thousands of people flocked to Bournemouth Beach despite warnings to stay away, leading to the declaration of a major incident. The beach reached its full capacity during the second day of a heatwave in the UK.

The area experienced traffic jams, altercations among visitors, and illegal overnight camping on the beach. Authorities urged attendees to "act responsibly" as temperatures soared to the mid-20s Celsius.

Traffic began to build up early on the roads leading to the coast, with some travellers journeying from as far away as Warwickshire. By Thursday evening, the Sandbanks peninsula was heavily congested, prompting the local council to reiterate their advice for people to "please stay away."

The declaration of a major incident activated a multi-agency emergency response to coordinate resources and address the challenges in the area.

England's Chief Medical Officer, Professor Chris Whitty, took to Twitter to address the alarming scenes that unfolded on Thursday, issuing a stern warning: unless the public adheres to social distancing guidelines, the relentless spread of COVID-19 could escalate dangerously.

Local council leaders echoed this sentiment, expressing their outrage over the reckless behaviour witnessed on the beaches. "We are horrified by the chaos on our shores," they stated emphatically. "The sheer irresponsibility exhibited by so many is shocking. Our emergency services are stretched to their limits, desperately trying to maintain safety. We have been compelled to declare a major incident and activate an emergency response."

The consequences of the day were stark, as the council recorded a staggering 558 parking fines. On Thursday morning alone, dedicated crews worked tirelessly to collect thirty-three tonnes of litter that marred the coastline, with an additional eight tonnes picked up between the piers just the day before.

Bournemouth East MP Tobias Ellwood raised concerns on Twitter, urging the government to dispatch more officers to Dorset if needed to tackle the growing traffic chaos and antisocial behaviour. "It is deeply disappointing to witness selfish and dangerous actions by several individuals," he lamented. "While closing Dorset's beaches entirely was not a feasible option, we did post signs alerting visitors to overcrowding at railway stations and along the approaches to our motorways. The government's response to the overwhelming crowds at our beaches must be swift and decisive; otherwise, the lockdown measures will have been in vain. So please, for now, stay away from all our stunning seafronts."

In response to the unfolding crisis, additional police officers were mobilised, and strict security measures were implemented to protect refuse crews who faced intimidation and abuse while diligently clearing overflowing bins. Both the Royal Bournemouth Hospital and Poole Hospital declared a major incident, bracing themselves for the consequences of the overwhelming crowds.

Assistant Chief Constable Sam de Reya of Dorset Police voiced her concern via Twitter: "In these unprecedented times, people should stay away from our beaches. A surge of visitors to one area places an undue strain on our emergency services."

Television broadcasts showcased the disheartening reality of beaches and popular locales teeming with people, each crowded scene a stark reminder of the challenges posed by the current crisis.

On the sweltering second day of the UK heatwave, police in Hove took decisive measures by enforcing a dispersal order, prompted by a boisterous crowd that had gathered. Nearby, at Bournemouth Pier, a vibrant sea of humanity surged toward the glistening waves, with colourful inflatables bobbing in the water and families sprawled across the golden sand. Groups of revellers, far exceeding the limit of six, set up camp beneath shady gazebos, their laughter and chatter filling the air.

By mid-morning, the breathtaking park at Durdle Door was nearly bursting at the seams, teeming with visitors eager to soak in the sun. Amid the chaos, a dedicated volunteer tried valiantly to manage traffic, but found themselves on the receiving end of verbal insults and even spittle from an unruly individual, their frustration adding to the already charged atmosphere.

As government guidelines permitted households to journey to parks and beaches without restriction, both councils in Dorset anxiously implored the government to impose travel limits. They feared that such a surge of visitors could lead to a troubling spike in COVID-19 cases in their picturesque area.

Amidst this scene of overwhelming activity and disregard for social distancing, the sense of normalcy and respect seemed to vanish. Sammy, cocooned in her apartment, gazed out her window, her heart heavy with disgust and sorrow as she witnessed the chaos unfold before her.

Social distancing was virtually nonexistent, and there was a noticeable decline in normal, respectful behaviour.

Chapter 11

Judas Joe

Dorset Police, the council, and volunteers successfully restored order to the county, and she confidently decided it was time to head to the shops. Dressed in full personal protective equipment (PPE), including gloves, she was prepared for the outing.

As she approached her car, she instantly noticed that the door to the car park from the neighbouring block was opening *This cannot be happening. I hope it's not Debbie Downer or the Lady Botherer,* she thought to herself.

"Oh, Sam, I'm glad to see you. Can you believe what's going on? Have you seen behind the beach huts? People have turned them into toilets; it's disgusting!" Debbie Downer exclaimed, her eyes brimming with tears.

"Yes, it's been outrageous," Sam replied firmly as she opened the car door and took a step back from Debbie.

"My husband is currently out of work, and I can't contribute due to my bad knee," Debbie continued, her tone emphasising the weight of her situation.

You really need to step up! thought Sam, who had overcome her own injuries, PTSD, and broken bones. She couldn't help but think about the veterans she worked with, battling PTSD and living with amputations, as well as the incredible pressure faced by first responders and the NHS, who continue to push through.

"We are in a tough financial situation. I've had a falling out with my sister over it, my mother is on the at-risk list, and my husband's family has cut us off," Debbie declared, her expression a mix of frustration and sadness.

Quelle surprise! thought Sammy as she stood there getting GBH of the earholes.

"I remember you wanted to upgrade your kitchen during our coffee chat before all this chaos. Do you still want to go ahead with it? My husband has plenty of time to help."

Sammy did want to upgrade her kitchen, It was nine years old.

"I do, actually. Could he also provide a quote for spotlights in my lounge, office, and hallway ceilings, as well as a couple of extra sockets? Can he do electrical work?" Sammy asked.

"Of course, he can do anything you need. Just give me your number," she replied, her mood seeming to brighten.

After exchanging numbers with Debbie Downer, Sammy got into her car, hoping it might help alleviate Debbie's financial troubles.

Later that day, Debbie texted her, asking if her husband could come by to see the work and provide a quote.

They arranged for him to arrive at 7pm that evening, and Sleazy Weasley showed up promptly wearing a mask. He gave her a salute.

Idiot she thought.

Immediately, he started talking; the words that came out of his mouth were filled with vitriol, a cascade of venomous judgments about the concierge, fire marshals, second-home owners in the complex, and his neighbours.

"I am going to quote for the concierge/fire marshal contract; I could do a better job than they can. They have put us all at risk. They are criminally negligent. If someone gets COVID-19 here, it will be their fault. I will sue them for corporate manslaughter if my wife dies because of them," he droned on.

Sammy just let him vent.

"My wife is ill and very angry; I have to collect
our parcels now because she won't go in there. The
doctors are useless; you can't get an appointment.
The NHS is useless, and so is that idiot of a Prime
Minister," he lamented.

"I am concerned about your wife, which is why
I asked you to quote. She seems very distressed
about your financial position after you lost your job.
How are you holding up?" Sammy asked politely.

"I am pissed off. We would sell up, but it seems
that 99% of the people here have lost money
when they sold. The prices have fallen, not risen,
here; something is not right about that. That
Directions Property woman is corrupt, selling
the apartments off cheap. It wouldn't surprise
me if she is buying them herself to increase her
portfolio. Her rental prices are too low, too, which
means she is a slum landlord, and that gives us
slum tenants. Her offices are right in Boscombe,
which is a dodgy area full of drug users and
prostitutes. She has a monopoly on this place; her
brochures are in the concierge office, but no other
estate agents have them. Stan in the concierge told
me that, and I bet she doesn't do any background
checks on the tenants. She just wants the money,
that's all. Have you seen her with her bleached
blonde hair, driving around in a Porsche, acting
like she owns the place? Her staff wear skirts
like fanny pelmets; it's disgusting. She even
got herself on the residents' association. She's

probably sleeping with a few of them. My wife is good friends with the cleaners, and they tell us everything about this place. Did you know people are smoking drugs, dropping litter, and someone was even running a brothel? Can you believe that? The residents are overfilling the bins and leaving sand in the corridors; they should wipe their feet before entering. And have you seen that stocky guy with the tattoos? He lives above us, and I bet he's the one smoking cannabis. He has loud parties, too. Dan, the black guy beneath us with the foreign girlfriend, told us that when we moved in," he angrily spewed.

She noticed the large purple bags under his eyes and thought he looked thin.

"I keep to myself. It's beautiful in my block; I am the only one here most of the time, so it's lovely, quiet, and peaceful. I suppose we all have different experiences," she replied. *"What a bitter and twisted individual,* Sammy thought to herself.

"Well, it's alright for you. You have a view of the sea; we don't. I will email your quote to you. Can I have your number, and could you send me your email address?" he added.

"Of course. Are you available for handyman-type jobs? I need some furniture assembled," she inquired, maintaining a neutral expression.

"Yes, I can do anything. I have a 3D printer in my workshop. You have some nice art. Do you need any pieces for the hallway?" His eyes seemed to light up.

"I actually do. I will send you some ideas if you would like to provide a quote," she replied, thinking about the motivational quotes she regularly posted on her LinkedIn page.

"Are you a qualified electrician?" she asked.

"Yes, of course," he stated.

"If I approve the quote for the kitchen, can you start in August if lockdown restrictions allow?"

"Yes, that would be fine. I work from 8am to 4pm, Monday to Friday, with an hour for lunch," he told her.

"How long will it take?" she asked.

"About two weeks," he replied.

"And can you take the old kitchen to the tip? It won't fit in my car."

"Yes, of course. That's included in the quote," he responded.

"Great, thank you," she said.

Sammy saw him out and consoled herself with the thought that at least she could lock herself in the office and put in her earbuds the next time he came. What a toxic person—just like his wife. Birds of a feather flock together.

Sammy regretted giving Debbie Downer her number. Debbie would send her daily messages about her life, detailing her woes, the pain she was experiencing, her falling out with an alcoholic friend, complaints about concierges violating COVID-19 regulations, and her struggles to find a parking space. It seemed endless.

Polite as ever, Sammy replied, "Please don't text me; I am at work."

As she pondered Debbie's parking situation, she recalled that Debbie only had one parking space for two cars, forcing her to ask the concierge nearly every day for an extra spot.

Later that day, Sammy decided to help Debbie Downer and texted her again. "My neighbour in the penthouse next door has two spaces and is rarely here. I can ask him if you can use one of his spots. You may have to pay for it or give him a gift, but I'm happy to reach out."

"Oh, thank you so much! That would be much better than parking at the top end of the garage. I've fallen over a couple of times," Debbie responded.

"I think Dick in the concierge office uses that space all the time when my neighbour is not home.

I'm not sure if he has permission, though; the previous tenant didn't allow the staff to park there because he thought they were idiots. I will email my neighbour on your behalf; his space is closer to your door and the lift," Sammy added.

After emailing her neighbour and explaining that Debbie Downer was disabled and had difficulty accessing the lift, she received a prompt response allowing Debbie Downer to use the space—provided she sorted the details out with Dick.

Sammy forwarded the response to Debbie Downer, ending the message with, "Leave it with you."

Within the hour, another text arrived from Debbie Downer. "Dick has blocked it. I don't know what he said to your neighbour, but he told me I can't use the space. He is keeping it for himself."

"Okay, I'm not getting involved, but I'll ask Kian about his space for you. It's never used," Sammy replied.

As she texted Kian, Sammy made a mental note to steer clear of neighbourly disputes in the future. Good fences make good neighbours.

"Can Debbie Downer use your parking space?"

"Of course, as long as she supplies me with a bottle of Jameson's regularly!" came the reply.

Sammy texted Kian Debbie Downer's number and added, "Leave it with you."

"She better not want to be my friend... lol," Kian responded, followed by another message.

"Can you take me to the shops... pleeeaaassssee?"

"No, sorry, I am working. But I'll be going to the shops at 7:30am tomorrow. If you want to come, meet me at Miss Silver."

"Okay, see you tomorrow! I've missed you, my Bournemouth sister!"

She smiled to herself as she got out the painting materials and began to work on the hallway. It was dark because there was little natural light, but the spotlights would brighten it up. The current kitchen had dark wood, so she had chosen white for the new one. That would help lighten the room, along with the 15 spotlights in the lounge, kitchen, and dining area, the 6 in the hallway, and the 6 in the office.

When the quote came through, she thought it was a bit steep but agreed anyway. She paid for the kitchen units herself after confirming with Sleazy that she could use his contractor discount with the suppliers.

Chapter 12

Remodelling

August was hot, the world was still chaotic, and she was keeping to herself. She missed Anna and the kids. They were staying in touch, and now that a bubble had been introduced, she included Anna in it; she was eager to catch up in person.

"Sleazy Weasley," as Kian had nicknamed him, arrived to start the remodel at 8am on Thursday morning, wearing a mask.

"Where are you going to start?" she asked.

"The kitchen," he replied.

"Great. If you need anything, I'll be in my office."

She went into her office and let him get to work.

"Has Sleazy Weasley arrived? You poor thing! PMSL," Kian texted.

"Come over for lunch; it's a beautiful day."

"Okay, see you at 1pm."

She kept herself busy until 1pm, then went over.

"How are you holding up? This pandemic has
been really tough; I understand why you're
not going into work—people's behaviour can
be so unpredictable right now. It's completely
understandable to be scared of catching COVID-19.
I appreciate your proactive approach in looking for
another job, maybe at a hotel. I'd be happy to help
you write a CV," Sammy said.

"I admire your computer skills; I feel so lost with
technology. I really should learn how to use them,"
Kian said thoughtfully.

"Have you thought about going back to college? It
would be great for you, especially since they should
be reopening in September," Sammy suggested
gently.

"That sounds like a good idea. I really miss Auntie;
she hasn't been over in so long. I miss my mom and
dad too," he said, his voice full of longing.

Kian immersed himself in the warmth of
the kitchen, his hands deftly moving as he
orchestrated a delightful culinary experience. The
tantalising aromas of freshly cooked tapas wafted
through the air, mingling with the faint scent of the
sea. Within moments, he had elegantly arranged
a colourful spread on the table, accompanied by a
bottle of 19 Crimes—her favourite wine, glistening
in the afternoon light.

"Oh, lovely! Thank you," she exclaimed, her eyes sparkling with appreciation as the golden rays of the sun danced over the bay, casting a warm glow on everything around them.

They settled onto the deck, the gentle breeze rustling the leaves and bringing with it the sounds of waves lapping against the shore. Their conversation flowed effortlessly from one subject to another, touching on families, friends, the unsettling state of emergency in Bournemouth, the Black Lives Matter movement, the sobering COVID-19 statistics, and the perplexing behaviour of the concierge and fire marshals.

"That Dick should really know his place; he is utterly vile. Can you believe he still lives with his mother? Bejesus, Samantha, the man is in his fifties and the epitome of a misogynist! And don't get me started on what he did to Debbie Downer over the parking space next door—that really reveals his true nature. She is disabled, and yet he acted like a selfish bastard," Kian exclaimed, his eyes blazing with indignation.

"That's absolutely disgusting," Sammy replied, her voice rising in frustration. "They should all be using the public car park instead of clogging up the residents' spaces. The concierge staff and fire marshal's vehicles create a constant blockade outside the concierge office, leaving no room for residents to pull in for their parcels or keys. The chaos is maddening! Some of them even park on the zebra crossing—it's not only unlawful, but it's also incredibly dangerous. Kids come barreling down the steps, giddy with excitement at the sight of the sea and beach, and they often dart across the zebra crossing without glancing. If a large van is parked over the crossing, you can't see whether anyone is waiting to cross; it's a disaster waiting to happen. The concierge should be managing the parking, but it seems they're doing absolutely nothing!" Sammy retorted, her voice laced with exasperation.

"You're absolutely right; they should really make use of the public parking lot right next door. Such lazy bastards," Kian scoffed, shaking his head in disbelief. "Did you hear about Dick? His car was smashed into during the state of emergency by some random fool who thought it was a good idea to sneak through our gates just to find a parking space. And get this, a woman actually spat at Stan!"

"No, I hadn't heard a word of that," Sammy replied, raising an eyebrow. "But honestly, even if I had the Hubble Telescope, it would take more than a cosmic lens for me to find anything remotely interesting about those people—especially that old fishwife and her absolute imbecile of a husband. So, what's the scoop? How did you find out?"

Kian couldn't help but burst into giggles at the mention of the old fishwife. "The old fishwife?"

"Gossip is the domain of the unintelligent," Sammy quipped, a playful smirk dancing on her lips.

Kian chuckled warmly, "You know how we Queens are; we thrive on a little gossip now and then!"

As Sammy stepped into her apartment at 5 PM, a wave of excitement washed over her. She gazed in amazement at the sight before her: most of the outdated kitchen had been completely dismantled, leaving a husk of what once was. The air was filled with the lingering scent of fresh paint and sawdust, a promising sign of the transformation to come.

Eager to catch up on her messages, she settled down at her desk and opened her email. Her heart raced as she spotted a new message from Chris, who was miles away in America.

"Oh, thank God he's alive!" she thought, a wave of relief washing over her like a warm embrace as her entire nervous system began to unwind.

With a heart full of gratitude, she typed her response, thankful that he had triumphed over whatever heavy shadow had been looming over him. She signed off playfully, "Stay in touch and never scare me like that again, or I swear, once the lockdown restrictions are lifted, I'll hop on a plane to the US and kick your ass!"

Later that evening, as she settled onto the couch with the soft glow of the television illuminating the dim room, she watched the news unfold. When she learned that AstraZeneca was making significant strides in developing a vaccine in the UK, hope surged within her like a bright light piercing through dark clouds, and she exhaled a deep, relieved sigh.

Yet, the pervasive trauma enveloping the world weighed heavily on her heart, its sadness sinking into her core. The nature of her work often placed her amidst grief and despair, and she reminded herself to care for her own mental well-being to prevent succumbing to vicarious trauma.

As she reflected on the troubling state of the world, feelings of disgust arose—not surprising given the self-serving and aggressive behaviours exhibited by some individuals. However, amidst the chaos, she found a wellspring of gratitude for those quietly working behind the scenes, tirelessly striving for the greater good.

On Thursday night, she stood on her balcony, joining her neighbours in heartfelt applause for the NHS. After a lovely afternoon spent sharing drinks with Kian, she felt slightly tipsy as she clapped along, feeling a mix of gratitude and solidarity. Understanding the impact of her stepmother's struggles with alcoholism, she made it a point to limit her drinking to just once a week. This careful choice stemmed from a deep desire to avoid repeating the patterns of her past, and she was resolute in her commitment to forging a healthier path for herself.

Sleazy arrived punctually at 8am on Friday morning, his demeanour lacklustre as he stepped through the threshold, tools in hand. He immediately got to work dismantling the old kitchen units, carefully unscrewing hinges and prying apart cabinets destined for disposal. Despite his early start, the process seemed to stretch on endlessly, with him moving at a sluggish pace that tested Sammy's patience.

"Goodness, he's so slow," Sammy mused to herself, frustration bubbling beneath her surface. Each drawer he pulled out seemed to take an eternity. She couldn't help but wonder if something was troubling him—was he experiencing some sort of existential malaise?

Unsatisfied with his lack of efficiency, her annoyance deepened when Debbie Downer, with her unmistakably gloomy aura, appeared at her doorframe.

"Hello! I just wanted to check on his progress," Debbie said in a chipper yet disconcerting way, her voice cutting through the air like a dull knife. "I'm here to help move the old kitchen items to the car and then to the waste facility."

Trying to mask her disbelief, Sammy shot her a skeptical glance. "I thought you were disabled and receiving Personal Independence Payments," she challenged, crossing her arms defensively.

"I am, and I absolutely do," Debbie retorted with a hint of smugness, an eyebrow raised as if she was victorious in a trivial debate.

Intrigued by the conversation, Sammy couldn't help but push further. "So, is your knee feeling better now?" she probed, genuinely curious about Debbie's alleged ailment and sudden burst of activity.

"No, I'm still waiting for an operation," Debbie Downer responded, her voice tinged with a hint of frustration.

Sammy leaned in, her brow furrowed with curiosity. "So, tell me, how can you support your husband when you're claiming Personal Independence Payment (PIP) due to your disability?" she asked, genuinely puzzled.

Debbie Downer's face flushed crimson as she fumbled for words, nervously stammering, "Well, it doesn't hurt today; the pain comes and goes, you know?"

Sammy observed her closely, feeling an unsettling sense of familiarity. She had quickly identified Debbie Downer's pattern of playing the "Victim" within mere hours of their first meeting. This strategy, she knew, was a hallmark of individuals who often seek attention rather than seek genuine help. Sammy's background in Transactional Analysis in Relationships had equipped her with the insights to recognise these manipulative behaviours, and she couldn't help but feel a mix of pity and frustration at the game being played before her eyes.

Transactional Analysis (TA) is a compelling and multifaceted theory of psychotherapy that was pioneered by the renowned psychiatrist Eric Berne during the dynamic 1950s. This innovative framework seeks to enrich our comprehension of human relationships by meticulously examining the intricate dynamics of communication patterns and interpersonal interactions, known as "transactions," Central to TA is the assertion that our personalities are structured around three distinct and essential ego states: Parent, Adult, and Child.

The Parent Ego State represents the beliefs, attitudes, and behaviours we have internalised from influential role models, including parents, teachers, and other authority figures. This state encapsulates the internalised voice of authority, often manifesting as nurturing or critical communications. The Adult Ego State, in contrast, embodies our capacity for rational and objective thinking, focusing on processing information and making decisions based on the present circumstances. It acts as a mediator that evaluates reality without the emotional influences of the other ego states. Finally, the Child Ego State reflects our emotional experiences from childhood, encompassing thoughts and feelings that range from playful and spontaneous to vulnerable and fearful.

TA effectively illustrates that all human interactions function as transactions—essentially reciprocal exchanges of communication between individuals. Each transaction comprises a stimulus, which serves as the initial message or query, and a response, which is the corresponding acknowledgment or reply from another individual.

Delving deeper into the rich landscape of Transactional Analysis, we uncover the concept of Complementary Transactions. These occur when the response aligns seamlessly with the expected ego state, facilitating clear and effective communication. For instance, if a person acts in a nurturing manner from their Parent Ego State and receives a receptive and appreciative response from another's Child Ego State, the interaction is smooth and harmonious. Conversely, we must also be mindful of Crossed Transactions, which arise when the responses deviate from anticipated expectations, leading to potential misunderstandings or conflicts. For example, if one person attempts to engage through their Adult Ego, but the other responds from their Child Ego State, the misalignment can disrupt effective dialogue.

Furthermore, Ulterior Transactions shed light on the more complex aspects of human communication, revealing the hidden motives or subtexts behind interactions. These transactions often involve a dual layer of messages: the overt message communicated and the covert message that may be manipulated for ulterior motives. This complexity deepens our understanding of how communication works, highlighting the rich tapestry of human interactions and the factors that influence them in both personal and professional realms.

Embracing TA provides us with invaluable insights into cultivating more fulfilling and positive relationships. It illuminates the concept of "games," which are repetitive social interactions that can inadvertently harm relationships and undermine self-esteem. Additionally, it introduces us to the notion of scripts—lifelong plans formulated in childhood that often govern our adult behaviours, sometimes without our conscious awareness.

In the therapeutic setting, TA practitioners employ various techniques to help individuals gain awareness of their ego states and interaction styles. Their goal is to empower clients to identify and understand their communication patterns, move away from negative games, and develop assertive, healthy communication skills. Ultimately, this leads to a more authentic and satisfying life journey.

Debbie Downer was in her child ego state and certainly had the capability to work. However, she seemed to prefer adopting a victim role to enjoy certain advantages. She succeeded in influencing the Department of Works and Pensions, her doctor, and likely many others too. Yet, Sammy saw through her façade. To Sammy, Debbie was simply a means to an end.

Sammy was inspired to breathe new life into her hallway with some vibrant artwork. She had gathered a collection of motivational quotes that resonated with her and decided to reach out to Sleazy, hoping he could bring them to life on canvas. Fortunately, this meant he wouldn't need to step foot in her apartment, allowing for a seamless creative collaboration.

With excitement, she shared the following uplifting quotes for him to transform into captivating pieces of art:

"There are three types of friends, friends for a reason, friends for a season and friends for a lifetime."

"Some people move our souls to dance. They awaken us to a new understanding with the passing whisper of their wisdom. Some people make the sky more beautiful to gaze upon. They stay in our lives for a while, leave footprints on our hearts & we are never ever the same again."

"To begin loving people today, we must close the door on the past. And that cannot happen without forgiveness! Forgive those who have hurt you - for your sake, not because they deserve it."

After two weeks of dedicated work, the kitchen transformation reached its grand finale, showcasing a sleek and modern aesthetic. The newly installed spotlights in the hallway and office bathed the spaces in a warm, inviting glow, illuminating every corner with clarity. The added electrical outlets, upgraded to USB-compatible sockets, offered a practical solution to the constant need for charging devices, enhancing the efficiency of daily life.

A week later, Sleazy arrived to deliver the first canvas, walking in with an air of self-satisfaction, until Sammy's keen eye caught the glaring spelling mistakes that marred the artwork.

"Oh, I apologise; I did not see that. I will create another version," he replied, his cheeks flushing a deep crimson as embarrassment washed over him.

Sammy silently criticised, "How could he overlook such fundamental errors?"

Eventually, the artwork was completed and proudly displayed, while her own vibrant painting found its place on the wall, filling the room with creativity and colour. The relief of parting ways with Debbie Downer and Sleazy was palpable; it felt as though a weight had been lifted, allowing her to return to a sense of normalcy. She settled the payment promptly, eager to close that chapter. However, within a week, she was dismayed to discover water seeping ominously beneath the sink.

In response, she swiftly composed a message to Sleazy, seeking assistance for the unexpected issue.

"The sink is leaking. How long is your work guaranteed for?" she inquired, her brow furrowed with concern.

"I'll come over and fix it tonight," he replied curtly, his tone lacking any enthusiasm.

As she leaned closer to inspect the sink, she noticed that the white sealant around the edges had begun to peel away, revealing a damp gap where water was steadily dripping.

He showed up exactly at 7 PM, looking weary and annoyed, carrying a large toolbox in one hand and a tube of fresh sealant in the other.

"Is the leak coming from the pipes beneath the sink?" she asked, hoping to pinpoint the issue.

"I didn't install those pipes," he protested defensively, crossing his arms.

"Well, you did fit the sink itself when you replaced it, didn't you?" she shot back, narrowing her eyes at him.

"I didn't install the original pipes," he insisted again, his frustration palpable.

"Just fix it, please. You put in the sink, and it appears to be too small for the opening. Plus, all of the sealant has come undone," she urged, casting a critical gaze at the mismatched installation.

He responded with an annoyed glare, his irritation evident on his face.

In that moment, she thought to herself, he can't handle criticism or take responsibility for his work. What a child.

She recognised the familiar manifestation of his child ego state, brimming with defensiveness and rebellion. Little did she know, this ego would resurface in dramatic fashion a little over a year later, ultimately involving herself, the police, and a judge in a whirlwind of consequences.

Chapter 13

September 2020

Sammy decided to join a dating site; it had been years since she had been in an intimate relationship, and she wanted to test the waters. She also desperately needed a hug.

Tentatively, she wrote her profile and posted a couple of pictures. It wasn't long before she had arranged a date with a RAF veteran who lived locally.

They met for coffee, and he seemed pleasant enough. A second date was arranged where he met with Kian and her at Kian's, and the three of them spent a pleasant evening on the deck.

The third date was a dinner date where he would cook for her at her apartment.

He arrived all flustered with a bag of food.

"I have had a right run-in with the staff at Tower Park. I took the kids bowling earlier, and I refused to wear a mask," he huffed.

"Oh, here we go!" She thought as he started to unpack the food.

"I couldn't find any Jack Daniels, so I got you Jim Beam instead.

"Oh, thanks, I don't like it," she said flatly. "Could have made an effort," she thought.

"You know, there are aliens everywhere, the Queen is an alien. She's a shape-shifter. Aliens are in the London underground and they are breeding and using humans as sex slaves," he said with a serious look on his face.

Sammy was highly amused and stifled her laughter.

"Oh really!" she responded.

"Yes, absolutely. Anyway, I told the staff at Tower Park we all have asthma, so we are not wearing masks. I have a fake document that says I have asthma; you can easily download it from the web. Want me to get you one? And I am certainly not having the vaccine, it's the government injecting us all with tracking serum. They have spies everywhere, they are in all our electronics, Siri and Alexa are spying on us all," he continued.

"Ok, do you smoke weed?" she quizzed him.

"Of course, do you, can I light up?" he asked.

"No, you can't, and you need to leave right now," she said, giving him her death stare.

She moved away from him.

"What? But I have brought all the food over!" He protested.

"You can take it with you, and the Jim Beam," she offered.

"Are you joking?" he asked.

"No, I am not joking." Then, adding, "We are not compatible, I hate drugs and the Queen is not a shapeshifter, please leave now."

He looked hurt, then angry, then he put his finger in his ear, as if connecting with an ear device and said, "I will return to HQ shortly."

"Oh my god, he is mad," Sammy thought to herself as he reluctantly collected the food and left.

She immediately texted Kian,

"Are you in? Can I come over?"

"Of course, bring wine!"

Sammy drove to the shops and bought several bottles of 19 Crimes and McGuigan's, and arrived still in shock at Kian's.

"What happened?" Kian asked with a look of concern on his face.

"Jesus, the guy was a lunatic, started going on about aliens and the Queen being a shapeshifter."

Kian collapsed in a fit of giggles.

"He seemed ok when he was here, Bejesus, you had a lucky escape!"

They sat on the deck as she gave him the details of the conversation.

"Bejesus, what a loon! You should have kept the Jim Beam. I would have had it. I am on Grinder and there are some right eeijits on there too, you have to be careful," Kian advised.

"I am never dating again, my Bournemouth Brother," she said.

"You should marry me, we would be grand together, but you have to let me have sex outside of marriage with men," Kian offered.

"Ok, deal, but you can never have sex with me, ever," she countered.

"Deal!" he said.

"Sláinte!" They both said, clinking their glasses together.

"Here's to a marriage of convenience," Sammy toasted.

Sammy didn't date again; she threw herself into her much safer work.

Opposite her apartment complex on the other side of the road were a row of apartments that looked cute, they were facing the ocean and multi-coloured in pastel pink, blue and cream. She thought the view must be amazing from there. She looked at the local estate agents to see if any were for sale, and to her delight, there were two. She made an appointment to view and was pleasantly surprised at how large they were.

The housing market was buoyant, and a sense of restlessness was likely the reason, or perhaps neighbours falling out over the pandemic. Sammy was curious as to how much her property was worth, so she got three estate agents to come and value it.

The property she had looked at over the road was on the market for £300,000.00. She decided to put her apartment up for sale. She wanted a change and did not need a concierge or a residents' gym.

Watching the news was still depressing; she avoided it as much as she could. Maybe once a week, she would watch it. She still regularly tested herself for COVID-19.

The apartment looked great, with a new kitchen, lots of light, and a fresh paint job. She had a few viewings but no buyers. Unfortunately, as she thought at the time, but what turned out to be for the best, it did not sell.

She wondered about renting it out, and got a rental value of £1,700.00 a month, not too shabby.

Sammy liked to have options, and she saw in the paper that the Barbados Government was offering a 12-month Welcome Stamp for people who could work remotely and provide for themselves financially. She mulled it over in her mind; it sounded like paradise to her, and she was all set up to work remotely.

Barbados first offered the 12-month Welcome Stamp on June 30, 2020. This new visa program allowed remote workers to live and work in Barbados for up to a year. The Barbados government announced the program in June 2020, and the Remote Employment Bill, 2020 was passed to give effect to it.

The only problem was that you couldn't leave Britain, as all the airports were locked down. Ah, well, she would just wait and see what the future held.

Looking back, she hadn't had a holiday since 2014, and she was used to travelling on her own and staying on her own. But what to do about Pawsey, her beloved cat? She considered the options of keeping her or rehoming her.

"I will have Pawsey, I love her, and you can get her back when you come home," Kian offered.

Problem solved. Sammy loved it when that happened.

"I will cook her fresh meals with her favourite meat and spoil her rotten, oh please let me have her!" Kian begged.

"Deal," Sammy smiled.

Chapter 14

Early Autumn Reunion

Work was getting busier, by the end of October, she had worked with 15 clients, 9 were through Phoenix, some were through private practice, and some through various charities. She was pleased to have invested in a website, and a peer from her training remembered her and sought her out for trauma-focused therapy for the charity she worked for.

Sammy was pleased; her private practice was growing despite the pandemic, and she was making some money after two years of hardly anything coming in.

2018 had seen her take on only one client, and 2019 had seen her take on only three clients.

Kian joked with her, citing a line from the movie Field of Dreams.

"If you build it, they will come!"

Her clients were a mix of males and females, veterans, police officers and civilians, all of whom were affected by the pandemic, mentally and financially. Telephone and Zoom counselling became the norm.

Anna, Ewan, and Alfie finally visited, and they sat outside Kian's blue beach hut. It was still warm and sunny, but they were all well wrapped up. Sammy loved her North Face jacket and beanie hat, just the perfect gear for sitting outside as the weather cooled.

"What a nightmare this has been," Anna said with a heavy sigh.

"Horrible, I have missed you," Sammy replied, giving her a hug.

"We missed you, Aunty Sam," said Ewan, biting into his ham sandwich.

Sammy had made a packed lunch for them all and brought her cool box full of food down to the hut.

"Have you got some prawn cocktail crisps?" Alfie asked.

"Sure, in the box, mate, I know they are your favourite," Sammy winked at him, noticing how tall he had grown since she last saw him.

Alfie looked like he had won the lottery as he pulled out the crisps and a banana milkshake.

"No one wants to go out anyway, too scared of getting stabbed. Bournemouth is evil these days, and look at London, it is getting worse," said Ewan.

Sammy's heart sank to hear a 16-year-old boy tell her he feared going out in his home county was truly heartbreaking.

"My mates in Blandford go out in groups for protection, so many kids are carrying knives now. I am not, though, Aunty Sam. When I get my car next year, will you teach me to drive?" Ewan smiled at her.

"Sure, I will. Have you applied for your provisional yet?" Sammy asked.

"Yes, there is a 6-month waiting list to do the online exam," he told her in between bites.

"I need to upgrade my passport, too, if I am going to Barbados."

"Are you really going to go?" Alfie asked.

"Yes, it seems like a wonderful opportunity. Kian is going to look after Paws, so I just need to get vaccinated and wait for the airports to open. Barbados is on the red country list, so I don't think it will be anytime soon, but I have got the Welcome Stamp now, it won't come into effect until I travel."

"I don't blame you, I would go if I were you," Anna said, then added. "We will come over and visit you once you are settled."

"Brilliant idea," Sammy smiled at her friend.

"I have been looking at the food prices, it is extortionately expensive, I will lose weight too, I don't eat much in the heat, and it will be hot!" Sammy said wistfully.

"You don't need to," said Anna

"I think I am developing Covid Curves," Sammy laughed; she was aware she had gained weight.

"Are you coming for Christmas this year?" asked Anna

"Well, I can't this year, as it breaks COVID-19 regulations. Your mom is one household, Mia and her boyfriend are another household, and your boyfriend is another one. I don't want to be giving or receiving COVID-19 for Christmas," Sammy raised her eyebrows.

"Oh gosh yes, you are right, I will save you some Turkey," Anna said.

After lunch, Alfie played on his skateboard and Ewan went for a paddle. Sammy and Anna sat in silence, looking at the ocean, both lost in their thoughts, united in their fear and worried about their futures.

"When do you finish University?" Sammy asked.

"Got another year to go, this year was awful, online lectures are not the same, and I miss being with people," Anna replied, looking sad.

"I know what you are saying, I miss people too. How is Mia now she is living with her boyfriend?" Sammy questioned her friend.

"They seem ok, I think she is glad to get away from the boys!" Anna laughed as she responded, then added. "Any luck with the sale of your apartment?"

"No, a few viewings but no offers," Sammy said with a sigh.

"I'll be moving to Bournemouth when Alfie leaves school, he's talking about going into the fire service," Anna informed her with a nod.

"I always thought he'd follow his dad into the army," Sammy replied.

"I don't want him to, but it's his life, he's such a good athlete, his football skills are amazing, he's missed that during this nightmare. Mother is lonely and struggling, and I'm so worried about her," Anna looked sad.

Sammy sensed her friend was sad; she was sad too, but they held their stiff upper lips and watched the boys playing on the beach.

"How's work?" Anna broke the silence.

"Busier, I've had 15 clients this year so far, Phoenix have been great. They do exactly what they say they're going to do. I'm impressed they're managing to raise money in this nightmare. I've met some incredibly strong people, I do love my work, haven't made any profit yet, not even broken even, but they say that takes five years," Sammy told her friend.

"I think you're amazing, Sam, I couldn't do it," Said Anna.

"I was surprised you didn't continue after Level 3, I missed you on Level 4, it wasn't the same without you," Sammy told her.

"There's no money in counselling, that was the reason I changed paths into Law, I've kids to support and an aging mother," Anna replied.

"It's hard, isn't it? I didn't have to support my parents, thank goodness. Both are dead now, but I did pay my mother's mortgage off for her in the nineties. I never heard a word from her civil partner after she died, not an offer of anything. I would have liked her engagement and wedding ring from my father, she never took them off, you know. And you know all about the gold digger and my father, Jesus, she is a vile woman, not content with a forty-three million pound estate, she had to take the house my father let me live in away too.

Money is the root of all evil, my friend. Ensure that you have your financial affairs in order for your children. Do not die intestate and be careful of any man who comes into your life. There are many gold diggers out there, male and female."

Sammy had come to terms with her family history.

"I can't believe how greedy she was and how you were treated all your life by your father's women, and your own mother, I could never leave my kids, not ever," Anna said as she watched Alfie & Ewan.

"He was a domestic violence perpetrator, Anna. I don't blame her for leaving him, and she probably thought Ian and I would be better off as he was wealthier. She didn't have the means to fight for custody of us, she was a lovely woman. I think she was strong to leave him after he beat her up. Every woman he married or lived with he beat up, or raped or controlled. I am proud of her for getting out when she did. It was the sixties and seventies, and a lot of women just put up with domestic violence and coercive control, thank God, times have changed," Sammy informed Anna.

Sammy had long got over the anger towards her mother. It had been part of her PTSD and grieving.

"True, have you seen the #MeToo movement?" Anna asked.

The #MeToo movement is a social movement that addresses sexual abuse, sexual violence, and sexual harassment, particularly in the workplace. It gained widespread attention in 2017 after allegations against Harvey Weinstein surfaced. The movement gained momentum through the use of the hashtag #MeToo on social media, where individuals shared their experiences of sexual harassment or abuse.

The phrase "Me Too" was initially used by activist Tarana Burke in 2006 to support survivors of sexual violence. However, it gained widespread popularity in 2017. The movement was sparked by articles in the New York Times detailing the sexual misconduct of Harvey Weinstein. Actress Alyssa Milano's call for women to share their experiences with #MeToo on social media led to a massive surge in participation.

The movement aims to raise awareness about sexual harassment and abuse and empower survivors to come forward and demand accountability from perpetrators. It also aims to address systemic issues that enable sexual violence. The #MeToo movement has led to increased public awareness and discussions about sexual violence,

Numerous high-profile figures are losing their jobs due to accusations of sexual misconduct, renewed efforts to seek justice for survivors through legal means, workplace reforms and investigations into sexual harassment policies.

"Yes, and I think it is wonderful, men who harass, rape, assault or beat on women are not men, they are little boys, insecure and egotistical and I would love for the justice system to partner them with someone male, twice their size and weight and give them a dose of their own medicine," Sammy told Anna.

"That would be justice," Anna agreed.

"I am working with a couple of survivors of domestic violence; they are strong women, I love working with them. You are a strong woman too Anna Banana, you didn't take any shit from your ex," Sammy said, smiling at her friend.

"Thanks Sam, love you," Anna replied.

"I often think counselling training is for the wealthy, it costs a fortune to qualify, have personal therapy and do the hundred voluntary hours, and I still get organisations asking me to volunteer, the cheek," Sammy looked annoyed.

"It will all work out for you, Sam, just give it time, my lovely," Anna smiled at her.

Alfie went by on his skateboard, grinning to himself as Ewan came back and sat down with them.

"Are there any ham sandwiches left?" he asked.

"In the cool box, there are milkshakes and crisps too Ewie," Sammy replied.

It felt so good to be sitting with her friends again after so long, looking out over the ocean and hearing the sounds of the waves crashing on the shore.

"Shall we have a get-together at mine for our Birthdays? You could stay over?" Sammy asked Anna.

"Sounds like a plan, I will see what weekend I am free, and if Alfie is at his dad's, how about the 23rd January, it's a Saturday, that would be right in the middle of our birthdays?" Anna grinned.

"Great, you are in my bubble, so it will be ok for us to be inside," Sammy smiled.

Ollie, her neighbour, came walking towards them with his French Bulldog.

"Heya mate! How are you?" He smiled warmly at her.

"Heya, I haven't seen you for a while, enjoying the apocalypse?" She responded.

"Nightmare, mind if we join you?" Ollie asked.

"Sure, we can make a bubble," Sammy said as he got his chair out of his beach hut and sat with them.

The friends sat until sunset, watching the ocean, and then reluctantly said goodbye to each other.

It had been a beautiful day.

Chapter 15

The Grenadier Guards Iraq, Afghanistan & Repatriation.

In mid-October, Gary from Phoenix called her.

"I have a Gren Guard for you, Sam; he is in a bad way. "Can you do your thing?" he asked

They had built up a trusting relationship over the year, and Gary trusted her to get in touch with clients as soon as practicable.

The Grenadier Guards (GREN GDS) proudly holds the esteemed position of the most senior infantry regiment in the British Army, leading the Infantry Order of Precedence with honour. Their historical roots stretch back to an impressive 1656, when Lord Wentworth's Regiment was established in Bruges to safeguard the exiled Charles II. In 1665, this regiment united with John Russell's Regiment of Guards, forming what we now know as the 1 Regiment of Foot Guards. Over the years, the

Grenadier Guards have played vital ceremonial, protective, and operational roles, exemplifying dedication and excellence in service. Their legacy is truly remarkable!

In 1900, the regiment proudly contributed a cadre of personnel to establish the esteemed Irish Guards, and in 1915, it also played a vital role in forming the Welsh Guards.

The regiment's rich early history is filled with remarkable engagements, as it participated in significant conflicts such as the War of the Spanish Succession, the War of the Austrian Succession, the Seven Years' War, and the Napoleonic Wars. At the close of this illustrious era, the regiment was honoured with the "Grenadier" designation by a Royal Proclamation.

During the Victorian era, the regiment continued its legacy of bravery by taking part in pivotal campaigns, including the Crimean War, the Anglo-Egyptian War, the Mahdist War, and the Second Boer War.

In the First World War, the Grenadier Guards expanded impressively from three battalions to five, with four valiantly serving on the Western Front. The Second World War saw the formation of six battalions, some of which transitioned to an armoured role within the Guards Armoured Division, actively participating in theatres of conflict across France, North-West Europe, North Africa, and Italy.

Post-Second World War, the regiment transitioned from three battalions to two, and then to one battalion by the mid-1990s. Major deployments during this period have encompassed essential operations in Palestine, Malaya, Cyprus, Northern Ireland, the Gulf War, Afghanistan, and Iraq, exemplifying its unwavering commitment to service.

Her client proudly served for sixteen years and completed multiple deployments to Afghanistan during Operation Herrick, a critical phase of the British military's efforts in the war. They were specifically deployed to Helmand Province in 2007, 2009-2010, and 2012.

Their service based in Helmand Province, a critical conflict zone in southern Afghanistan. They were charged with the aggressive engagement of insurgents, specifically the Taliban, to dismantle their presence and fortify the development of Afghan security forces. The fighting in Helmand was fiercely intense, and the Grenadier Guards faced substantial casualties, including the loss of Lance Corporal Duane Groom in 2012.

During their 2012 tour, the Grenadier Guards decisively transferred control of additional areas to Afghan security forces, marking a significant step in the transition of responsibility.

She dialled the client's number and confidently stated, "This is Sam from Phoenix Heroes. How are you today?" They established a strong therapeutic alliance over 20 sessions, which continued through February 2021.

He had been deployed to Iraq and played a crucial role in the repatriation of the first female soldier shot down in a helicopter, alongside four male companions who also lost their lives.

This experience was one of the most distressing moments of his tour.

When Sammy asked, "How does this affect you in the here and now?" He responded firmly, "I still experience flashbacks. I can clearly see the coffins lined up, and it drives home the reality that war is a serious business—people die in horrific ways. The fact that she was a female soldier, the first one killed in action, is tragic and it fills me with anger."

"What have you done with your anger?" she asked.

"I'm not sure," he responded, his tone flat.

"You've likely internalised it, suppressed it, and turned it inward. That makes sense, doesn't it?" she asserted.

"I can be quite moody and often become aggressive in an instant," he admitted.

"You are trained to kill, and if someone does flick your switch, you can go from 0-60 in a millisecond, that's what training does to soldiers. They are not trained to sit around the campfire and sing 'Ging Gang Goolie,' are they, mate?" she responded.

Then added, "It's OK to be angry; anger is a normal human emotion. I would be angry if someone shot my colleague with an RPG and killed them."

"I have nightmares about it, and I can still see the coffins all laid out," he told her, going deeper.

"Go into the nightmare, what is it that you want to say to her?" she asked.

"I am sorry this happened, you were so young and so brave, I wish I could have saved you, I will carry you in my heart always, my sister." With that, he let out a sob.

"It's ok to cry, that's what should happen, you can be sad and tears are a normal human reaction to grief, all humans have tear ducts, tears are a way of releasing emotions, we cry when we are sad, happy, frustrated or angry," she explained.

"We lost so many, it was awful," he said with tears in his voice, then added.

"I have a wife whom I love to the end of the earth, and daughters, I can't help but think about how her family would be feeling. I know how I would feel if I lost my wife or daughters."

He went silent for a long time.

Sammy held the silence and let him process his emotions.

"Do your other veterans cry in therapy ?" he asked.

'Absolutely, it's completely understandable to have such reactions in situations that are anything but normal. War creates an environment filled with unimaginable horror, hopelessness, and helplessness, making it incredibly difficult for those who endure it. Many veterans face societal pressure to simply "suck it up and carry on," while this approach may provide some short-term relief, it's so important to acknowledge that the feelings and memories associated with these experiences don't simply disappear. They can resurface later, often as painful triggers, night terrors, or flashbacks.

Our experiences are intricately recorded in the hippocampus of the brain, which also houses the amygdala, the part responsible for processing our emotional responses. In an effort to meet the weight of their responsibilities, many veterans find themselves suppressing these deep-seated emotions. However, this suppression often comes at a high cost. The memories tied to these emotions can resurface after months or even years, manifesting as a constant presence that can be incredibly challenging to cope with. It's vital to approach these feelings with compassion and understanding, recognising the profound impact they can have on a person's life.

The effects of this situation can be incredibly distressing, and it truly breaks my heart to witness so many veterans who feel isolated in their struggles. This internal battle can lead to numerous challenges, and, tragically, some may even consider ending their lives as a way to escape their overwhelming pain. It's essential to recognise their suffering and reassure them that they are not alone; there is support out there for them. We must foster an environment where veterans feel safe to express their experiences and seek the help they deserve," Sammy shared this with deep compassion.

"I understand now. Thank you, Sam."

"Are you feeling overwhelmed right now?" she gently asked, her voice filled with concern.

"Yes," he responded.

"Experiencing suicidal feelings can encompass a range of emotions, from having abstract thoughts about ending your life to feeling as though your loved ones would be better off without you. It might also involve contemplating specific methods of suicide or even making clear plans to take your own life.

If you're finding yourself in this dark place, know that it's completely normal to feel scared or confused by these emotions. They can feel incredibly overwhelming, and it's important to recognise that you're not alone in this struggle. Please remember that there is support available, and reaching out to someone you trust can be a vital step toward finding relief and healing."

"I often find myself contemplating jumping off a bridge," he asserted.

"Everyone experiences suicidal feelings in their own way, and it's important to acknowledge that. You might find it hard to cope with the overwhelming emotions you're facing. It may not necessarily feel like a desire to end your life, but rather an inability to continue living the way you are right now. These feelings can build up over time or shift rapidly from one moment to the next. It's completely natural to feel confused about why you're experiencing this. Please know that you're not alone in this struggle." Sammy expressed gently.

"I don't feel that way all the time; the pandemic isn't making it any easier," he asserted.

"You might be experiencing a deep sense of hopelessness, feeling as though there's no purpose in continuing on. It's natural to feel overwhelmed by negative thoughts or to struggle with unbearable pain that seems endless. You may feel as if you're not valued or needed by those around you, creating a sense of desperation that can make it hard to see any other way forward. It's not uncommon to feel disconnected from your own body or to feel numb in response to everything that's happening. These feelings can be incredibly heavy, and it's important to know that you're not alone in facing them," Sammy gently shared.

"I am not captivated by death," he said.

"It is understandable to experience a range of feelings that can be quite overwhelming. You might find yourself struggling with poor sleep, perhaps waking up earlier than you wish, and noticing changes in your appetite that can lead to weight fluctuations. It is common to feel a lack of motivation to take care of yourself, which may manifest as neglecting your physical appearance. You might also feel the urge to withdraw from social interactions or think about making a will and giving away possessions. Communicating these feelings can be difficult, and it is not unusual to grapple with self-loathing and low self-esteem, alongside urges to self-harm," Sammy expressed these feelings, highlighting a deep sense of sadness that many can relate to in challenging times," she explained.

"I have a few of those, yes, but I would never do that to my wife and kids," he responded quietly.

"I understand that the duration of suicidal feelings can vary greatly from person to person. It is common to feel as though happiness or hope will never be part of your life again. However, I want to emphasise that with the right treatment and support, including self-care, many individuals who have experienced these feelings can find their way to fulfilling lives.

I know that it can be incredibly difficult to open up about what you are going through. You may feel a strong desire for others to understand your struggles, yet feel unsure of how to share, worried about whether they will understand, fearful of being judged, or concerned that you might upset them. Please remember that you are not alone in this journey, and you deserve support. I am here for you, ready to provide assistance as you navigate through these challenging emotions. Let's make a suicide agreement verbally, you have to promise me you won't act on your thoughts in between our sessions," she told him.

"Ok, I promise," he replied.

"I will be sending you psychoeducation materials every week, designed to deepen your understanding of PTSD and provide you with effective management strategies. Each PDF will be rich with insights, giving you the tools you need as we move forward together. I'm pleased to let you know that Phoenix has generously funded

12 sessions for you. How does that sound?" she explained, her tone warm and encouraging.

"Brilliant mate, thank you, speak next week," her client answered.

In the course of his second session, he shared a poignant account of his experiences during Operation Herrick 6 in Afghanistan. He vividly described the devastating impact of improvised explosive devices (IEDs) on innocent civilians, particularly highlighting the plight of children caught in the crossfire of conflict. He reflected on the heartbreaking scenes he encountered, where families were torn apart and young lives were irrevocably altered by the violence. His words painted a stark picture of the challenges faced by those living in war-torn regions, emphasising the urgent need for awareness and support for the affected communities.

"Any particular one stand out?" she asked.

"It was utterly horrific to witness the devastation that IEDs inflict on human lives, especially on the innocent faces of children and the delicate forms of women. That was the most heart-wrenching aspect. I could see massive, gaping wounds tearing through their bodies, evidence of unimaginable violence. One particular scene remains etched in my memory: a man inside a white transit vehicle. When I lifted the tarpaulin, the sight was chilling—I could see straight through him, as if he were a ghost suspended between life and death. The entire moment felt surreal, as if I had stepped into a nightmarish dreamscape, detached from reality and grappling with the enormity of it all," he disclosed.

"Dissociation is a fascinating yet complex phenomenon," she began, her voice steady and insightful. "It's that eerie sensation where the world around you feels strangely unreal, as if you're observing your own life from a distance. This experience can manifest in two distinct forms: depersonalisation and derealisation, both of which are remarkable defence mechanisms that your brain employs to shield you in times of distress. Essentially, your mind is hard-wired for survival, instinctively reacting to overwhelming stressors, especially during traumatic events. Dissociation serves as a protective cloak, allowing you to momentarily escape the weight of reality, offering a means to navigate through the chaos of heightened emotions." she explained.

"Yes, that's exactly it," he sighed.

"Everyday moments of dissociation can often sneak up on us in unexpected ways. Picture this: you dive into the pages of an enthralling book or become captivated by a gripping film, so much so that the outside world fades away, leaving you in a cocoon of imagination where time seems to stand still. Or consider the experience of driving along a well-trodden path, the familiar sights blurring together, as you arrive at your destination without a recollection of the journey—lost in thought, your mind drifting to distant realms while your hands expertly navigate the steering wheel." she expounded.

"That's happened a lot!" He said with relief in his voice.

"Experiences of dissociation can vary greatly in duration, sometimes lasting just a few hours or days, but they can also extend for much longer periods—ranging from several weeks to multiple months or even years," Sammy explained. "During these times, individuals may feel disconnected from their thoughts, feelings, or sense of self, making it challenging to engage with reality as they typically would," Sammy explained.

'Really? That would make sense," he responded.

"Dissociation can manifest as a fleeting escape during moments of intense trauma, a protective mechanism that allows you to temporarily distance yourself from the overwhelming reality around you. Yet, for some, this response may have evolved into a learned habit—a refuge cultivated over years to shield oneself from the weight of stressful experiences. It might feel as if this practice has been a part of your life for as long as you can remember, quietly shaping the way you navigate the world," she continued.

"I did dissociate a lot when I was a kid," he said.

"Derealisation is a dissociative experience
that creates a profound sense of unreality or
disconnection from one's environment. Individuals
may find themselves enveloped in a surreal,
dreamlike state where they feel as though they
are observing their life from a distance, much
like a spectator in a film. This experience can
include vivid distortions of visual and auditory
perceptions, such as colours appearing muted
or sounds seeming far away and muffled. Those
affected may describe their surroundings as
alien or ethereal, perceiving everyday objects
as distorted or lacking their usual significance.
During these moments, it can feel as if they are
merely existing outside their bodies, leading to
a disconcerting sense of being unanchored from
reality and not fully engaging with the present
moment," she explained.

"That's exactly it, like I was in a movie," he told her.

"Oooo! Can I get your autograph?" she quipped.

They both burst out laughing.

"Laughter is a powerful tool for easing trauma
and serves as a wonderful release in tense
conversations.

Depersonalisation is a dissociative experience
marked by a profound sense of disconnection

from oneself. Imagine a sensation where your thoughts, emotions, sensations, and actions seem to float away, leaving you in a state of detached observation, as if you are an outsider peering into your own life. This can create a surreal, dreamlike atmosphere where the world around you feels oddly vague and disorienting, transforming everyday reality into an unfamiliar landscape.

In this state, individuals often feel as though they are gazing at their existence from a distance, as if they are trapped behind a glass barrier, watching their life unfold without truly participating in it. This detachment can lead to a diminished sense of individuality and identity, making the person feel like a mere shadow of themselves.

Despite this disconnection, individuals experiencing depersonalisation retain a crucial awareness: they understand that their feelings of detachment do not alter the reality around them. Unlike delusions, where one might mistakenly accept distorted perceptions as undeniable truths, those with depersonalisation recognise that their surreal experience stems from their own perception. Furthermore, it is essential to note that depersonalisation is distinct from derealisation, which involves a sense of unreality in the external world rather than within oneself," Sammy stated.

"Yes, I get it now, that's what happens, I go off somewhere in my head," he disclosed.

"Absolutely, I understand your feelings. It can be challenging, but it's important to embrace those defence mechanisms you have. They're like protective shields that have formed to keep you safe in difficult situations," Sammy said softly, her voice was calm and nurturing, as if she were guiding him through the stormy seas of his emotions.

"Think of them as loyal friends who help guard your heart, steering you away from harm while you navigate through life's challenges," Sammy informed him.

Chapter 16

It'll be lonesome this Christmas without you.

Christmas Day was different for Sammy this year; she spent it at home watching TV. The beach was quiet, with just a few people scattered here and there, and the usual Christmas Day swimmers were nowhere to be seen.

Sammy hadn't bothered to get any special food for the holiday since she didn't celebrate Christmas and wasn't a Christian.

Christmas Day, celebrated annually on 25th December, is a Christian holiday that commemorates the birth of Jesus Christ. For many people worldwide, it is a time for religious observance, festive celebrations, and cultural traditions.

Christians honour the birth of Jesus, the Son of God, through church services, prayers, and readings of the Christmas story. Additionally, Christmas Day is also recognised as a secular holiday, characterised by traditions such as exchanging gifts, decorating homes with lights and trees, and enjoying memorable meals with family and friends.

While most countries observe Christmas on 25th December, Eastern Orthodox Churches celebrate it on 7th January.

She reflected on her en-suite bathroom and realised she had never liked the tiles; it was time for an update. Since the apartment was still on the market, she believed that a renovation could make it more appealing to potential buyers.

Over the holidays, she emailed Sleazy, asking him for a quote to retile the bathroom, install a waterfall shower, and replace the toilet and sink unit.

Having already selected the shower, tiles, and sink unit, she included the supplier's link in her message and mentioned that she would purchase the materials herself, so she only needed a quote for the labour.

Sleazy responded promptly with a quote. Although it was slightly higher than she had hoped, she understood that finding a contractor during COVID-19 was challenging. She thought, "Better the devil you know," and decided to move forward.

They arranged for him to begin the work in early January.

____

By 31st December 2020, the deaths attributed to COVID-19 stood at 1,813,188. Yet preliminary estimates suggest the total number of global deaths attributable to the COVID-19 pandemic in 2020 is at least 3 million, representing 1.2 million more deaths than officially reported.

Chapter 17

2021

Sleazy arrived to start work looking as miserable as ever. The dark bags under his eyes had grown even larger, and he had lost more weight.

"I'll be in my office if you need anything. But before you begin, could you let me know if you can hear anything? The wall of the en-suite is shared with my office wall. I'm going to start speaking at my normal volume, so tell me if you can hear me," she said.

"Okay, this situation is so depressing," he muttered.

Sammy waited for him to go to the ensuite and then began to talk. She texted Sleazy, "Can you hear me?"

"No," he replied.

Confidentiality is essential in the therapeutic alliance. She had earbuds that she used while working, so if he could hear anything, it would only be her voice and not her clients'. Still, she wanted to ensure he wasn't listening in on her sessions—a precaution she deemed necessary.

She allowed him to start working and then focused on her own tasks, as she had six clients scheduled for the day. Sleazy was quite slow in completing the work, but the end result looked great. Additionally, he replaced the separate sink and toilet in the bathroom to match the unit in the ensuite. Sammy paid him immediately.

In January, Phoenix Heroes successfully processed three clients who were each serving members of the Army, Navy, and Air Force. Each of these individuals brought unique backgrounds and experiences, reflecting their dedication to service. Phoenix Heroes provided tailored support and resources, ensuring that each client received the assistance they needed for their specific situations and goals.

Anna and Ewan arrived on Saturday 23rd, bringing a wave of excitement with them for a cozy birthday celebration. The atmosphere was filled with warmth and joy as laughter echoed through her home, making it feel even more inviting. It was a true delight to have them there, and as the evening progressed, they shared stories and memories under the soft glow of candlelight. After a delightful night of festivities, they stayed overnight, leaving behind a sense of cherished moments and lasting friendships.

On Sunday evening, she made her way to the bin store in the car park to throw away her rubbish. As she walked, she realised it was the perfect opportunity to finally get rid of a large arc floor lamp that had been taking up space in her lounge. The lamp was an impressive piece, featuring a beautifully polished marble base that added significant weight to its structure. Standing as tall as she was, it arched elegantly, casting a warm glow across the room when lit. With a determined sigh, she decided it was time to part with this heavy yet striking fixture, ready to make space for something new.

As she walked back from the bin store, she encountered a male fire marshal named John, who was not wearing PPE. (Personal Protective Equipment)

"Can you help me lift a large lamp and bring it down to the bin store, please?" she asked him.

"Yeah," he replied.

Ok, I will see you outside my apartment in 5 minutes if that is ok?" she said.

He arrived 5 minutes later, still not wearing personal protective equipment (PPE). She had managed to move the lamp to the communal corridor.

"You put it in the lift and go down with it, I will use the stairs and see you on the ground floor," she told him. There was no way she was getting in the lift with him. She had on gloves and a mask.

Upon reflection, John could have taken the lamp to the bin store by himself, but assisting residents was not part of his responsibilities beyond fire marshalling duties.

To reach her bin store, she had to take the lift or use the stairs to go down two floors to the ground level. Then, she would exit her apartment building, walk across the courtyard, and descend two flights of stairs and through a fire door. After that, she needed to cross the car park and open the double fire doors to access the bin store. Her block was the only one without a lift to the car park, which made carrying large and heavy items challenging. Additionally, she had two disabled little fingers, making it even more difficult to carry bulky items.

John lifted the base, and she carried the top, and they walked to the bin store.

A CCTV camera is located on the opposite wall outside the bin store. It is the concierge's responsibility to ensure that the camera is functioning correctly. Additionally, the concierge must maintain accurate records of the CCTV footage, comply with GDPR regulations, and be a member of the Information Commissions Office.

Sammy opened the door and stepped inside, holding it open with her foot for John. He entered, and the door closed behind them. Together, they lifted the lamp and dropped it into the bin, which was about 5 feet high.

John looked her up and down like she was a piece of meat and said, "Could I have a hug?"

Sammy confidently stepped back through the double fire doors, positioning herself directly in the view of the CCTV camera, and shouted, "No, you cannot!"

John turned, walked past the camera, and headed up the ramp toward the concierge office, whistling. Sammy, horrified, returned to her apartment and called her police colleague.

After calming her down, she reported John to the police, the Residents Association, DFSB Ltd., and PMB Property Management.

Not only did he make an inappropriate sexual advance, but he also accosted her without wearing proper personal protective equipment (PPE). Sammy was disgusted by his behaviour.

In her formal complaint letter, she requested several key pieces of information: a copy of the CCTV footage related to her incident, the specific license numbers associated with the CCTV system, and a clear outline of the complaints procedures.

Despite her reasonable requests, she was met with silence from DFSB Ltd., leaving her feeling frustrated and ignored. After allowing a couple of weeks for a response, she decided to follow up with PMB Property Management through email, hoping for some clarity.

To her disappointment, PMB Property Management responded with a series of evasive excuses that seemed to deflect their responsibility. They insisted:

- "We are not responsible for addressing this issue."

- "You will need to contact DFSB Ltd. directly because they are the ones who employ the fire marshals."

- "Unfortunately, the CCTV footage for that day is not available since the system was not operational at that time."

Each of these responses only added to her frustration, as she felt that neither company was willing to take ownership of the situation or assist her in resolving her concerns.

Feeling dissatisfied with the situation, Sammy took the step of filing a formal complaint against the agency. In response, PMB continuously denied any responsibility for the issues she raised and redirected her concerns to DFSB Ltd.

Following her complaint, Sammy became increasingly aware of an unsettling pattern. Whenever she left the building during Dick's shifts, he seemed to deliberately walk by her, maintaining an unwanted presence. For instance, as she made her way to the car park, Dick would invariably appear, casually strolling past her with a disconcerting air of nonchalance. On occasions when she entered the complex, she noticed him stepping out of the office, making it a point to walk down toward the ramp, almost as if he were waiting for her. The frequency of these encounters left her feeling increasingly angry.

While discussing the situation with her colleagues, she burst out laughing. *What a moron.* His response to her complaint was to put himself in her path. Was this an attempt to intimidate her? If it was, it wasn't working.

She reported him to Dorset Police for harassment, explaining the background, which included their failure to comply with COVID-19 regulations, the incident in the bin store, and the lewd behaviour of some members of his team.

The investigating officer got back to her shortly afterward, informing her that John, the fire marshal, had died of COVID-19, which meant the case of sexual harassment was closed. He advised Dick to stay away from her and suggested that she purchase a body-worn video camera and a ring doorbell. She took his advice, and the doorbell was installed. To her amazement, the following day, Dick appeared outside her home with his phone and took a photo of it. *What a cretin!* she thought.

She sent an email to DFSB Ltd, also including PMB Property Management and the Residents Association in the correspondence, seeking clarification regarding his unusual and perplexing behaviour.

The Residents Association promptly acknowledged her email, responding with a courteous message that indicated the issue fell outside their area of responsibility. In contrast, PMB Property Management and DFSB Ltd both failed to respond to her inquiry.

Chapter 18

Sandhurst & The Stocktons

Phoenix Heroes hosted vibrant fishing events for veterans throughout the UK, creating tranquil spaces where the healing waters aid those grappling with PTSD. These gatherings not only offered a therapeutic escape but also fostered a sense of camaraderie, allowing veterans to reconnect with one another and open up about their wartime experiences, should they feel comfortable doing so.

In July, Sammy was brimming with excitement as she prepared to attend the event at the picturesque Sandhurst Lakes. The thought of finally meeting Gary and Sue filled her with anticipation.

To mark this new chapter, Sammy had enlisted Sleazy to overhaul her bedroom. The plans included moving the wardrobes to a fresh location on the wall, gracefully relocating her small TV to hang from the wardrobe door like a modern artwork, and transforming her dressing table into two charming bedside tables, each with its own character.

She deliberately scheduled the renovations for the day of her trip to Sandhurst, as she longed to escape the shadow of Sleazy and his toxic presence. With a heavy heart but a determined spirit, Sammy left the door open for him as she drove through the sun-drenched streets towards Sandhurst in Guildford, Surrey, ready to embrace the warmth of new friendships and healing waters.

She instantly recognised Gary and Sue, and a wide smile broke across her face as she approached them, warmth radiating from her. Though she yearned to embrace them, the habit of social distancing held her back, so she maintained a respectful distance.

Surrounded by the shimmering blue of the lake under the brilliant sun, they sat in a peaceful spot, the sound of rustling leaves adding to the ambiance. Their conversation flowed effortlessly, filled with enthusiasm as they discussed the mission of the Community Interest Company (CIC), the impactful work they were doing, their dreams for a brighter future, and their reflections on the challenges posed by the pandemic.

Lunch was a delightful affair, catered on-site by a talented company, creating an inviting spread that tempted the senses. Among the participants were veterans representing The Marines, The Parachute

Regiment, and The Guards, each sharing stories of bravery and camaraderie.

The air was charged with excitement, and the energy was contagious, filling the gathering with an uplifting spirit that made every moment feel alive.

Sue was a radiant presence, exuding warmth and kindness that instantly put others at ease. Her keen intelligence shone through in every conversation, and her deep passion for helping veterans was evident in the tireless way she dedicated herself to their needs. Sammy felt an immediate connection to her, drawn in by her compassion and genuine spirit.

Gary was everything she expected him to be: a professional Warrant Officer. Army warrant officers require a diverse skill set that includes technical expertise, leadership, communication, and adaptability. They often serve as specialists or technical advisors, possessing in-depth knowledge in specific areas such as aviation, maintenance, or logistics.

In addition to their technical skills, warrant officers must be strong leaders who can motivate, train, and mentor soldiers. Excellent communication, both written and verbal, is essential for advising, coaching, and effectively interacting with leaders at various levels. Furthermore, they need to be adaptable, capable of handling stressful situations, and possess strong problem-solving and decision-making skills.

Warrant officers are highly skilled specialists, often recognised for their extensive expertise and invaluable experience in their respective fields. They serve as the go-to authority for technical guidance, providing critical insights that can alter the course of operations. With a remarkable ability to learn new technologies and adapt to ever-evolving situations, they remain agile in the face of challenges.

In their vital leadership roles, warrant officers are entrusted not only with the motivation and inspiration of soldiers but also with the crucial task of fostering a united and cohesive unit. They are instrumental in cultivating an environment that promotes positivity and camaraderie among team members, which is essential for overall morale and effectiveness.

Beyond their formal responsibilities, these seasoned professionals take on the significant role of mentors, actively guiding junior officers and non-commissioned officers (NCOs). They equip these future leaders with the knowledge and skills they need to assume leadership roles with confidence and expertise. This mentorship is crucial for both individual growth and the long-term success of the unit.

Warrant officers often engage in strategic planning and play critical roles in risk management and project management. They analyse ongoing operations to ensure that the unit meets its overall objectives efficiently and effectively. Their ability to communicate clearly and persuasively with personnel at every level is paramount, as they must provide precise instructions, constructive feedback, and informed advice that can influence the success of missions.

Active listening forms the foundation of their communication skills. Warrant officers must genuinely understand the concerns and suggestions of their team members, effectively addressing any issues that arise, whether they are operational challenges or interpersonal conflicts. By fostering strong relationships with their subordinates, peers, and superiors, they build a culture of trust and cooperation essential for team success.

When confronted with crises or high-pressure situations, warrant officers must exhibit quick thinking and decisive action. They are trained to remain calm and focused, assessing situations rapidly to identify problems and formulate sound judgments. This ability to maintain composure under duress not only aids in problem-solving but also sets a positive example for their team.

Determination plays a key role in the success of warrant officers. They approach their goals with persistence, remaining steadfast in the face of challenges and obstacles that may arise along the way. In addition, proficiency with computers and relevant software is increasingly vital in their roles, as technology continues to advance and shape military operations. This technical expertise enables warrant officers to utilise the latest tools for data analysis, communication, and operational planning effectively.

Gary's nickname was Badger.

Sammy would always call him Boss.

As the sun dipped below the horizon, casting a golden glow across the sky, Sammy made the decision to drive home. Feeling that it was improper to linger any longer, she approached Gary and Sue, their voices mingling with the whisper of the evening breeze. With a warm smile, she wished them both a pleasant evening, then turned, her heart lighter, and began her journey home along the winding road.

As the sun dipped lower in the sky, painting the horizon with hues of orange and pink, she drove down the motorway with the top of Miss Silver down, the warm breeze tousling her hair. Her favourite playlist filled the air, each note blending seamlessly with the hum of the engine and the rush of the wind.

Upon arriving home, she stepped into her cozy apartment, greeted by the sight of Paws perched elegantly on the bookcase in the hallway, her fur shimmering in the soft light.

"Come on, beautiful girl," Sammy called, her voice warm and inviting. Paws, ever the loyal companion, jumped down and trotted after her, brushing against her legs with a gentle nudge that spoke volumes of her affection.

As Sammy opened the cupboard, the familiar sound of Likelix being torn open sent Paws leaping eagerly inside, eyes wide with excitement.

"You crazy girl, Pawsey," Sammy chuckled, amusement dancing in her eyes as she retrieved a treat. She squeezed it onto a waiting plate, the rich scent wafting through the kitchen, before placing it on the floor for her delighted furry friend.

Chapter 19

LMG Design Ltd

Sammy walked into the bedroom to see what Sleazy had done and felt disappointed once again at the pace of his work; he was just so slow.

He had moved the built-in floor-to-ceiling wardrobes and screwed them into the opposite wall, but the fit was poor. There were noticeable gaps, and he hadn't sealed the space between the top of the wardrobe and the ceiling or between the side and the wall. It looked shoddy, and the doors were not hanging straight.

Additionally, there was now an exposed patch of concrete floor where the wardrobes had been moved, so she needed to order some Karndean flooring to cover it.

He had removed the built-in dressing table and the attached bedside table, while the other bedside table was free-standing. To make matters worse, he had left the debris in the communal hallway.

Idiot!, she thought.

She texted him to say that she would be ordering the Karndean flooring and asked if he could install it. He replied that he could.

Later in the week, he returned with the dressing table, which he had repurposed into a bedside table, and fitted it next to the wardrobe.

"I'm not going to bother with the new sockets on either side of the bed, and there's no need to install a socket for the TV; there's already one in there," she said.

"That's fine. I will need to run the TV aerial through the ceiling and install a new aerial socket up there. It will be inside the wardrobe, so you won't see it," he responded.

"That's fine. When do you think you'll be finished?" Sammy asked, eager to have him out of her property as soon as possible.

"Next week, after the flooring arrives. It will be done then," he scowled at her.

What a moody, miserable git!, she thought.

"When are you taking the rubbish? It's a fire hazard being left in the hallway," she inquired.

He sarcastically replied, "Oh, I don't take rubbish," and then walked away.

Later that evening, she opened the en-suite vanity unit and noticed water leaking onto the shelf.

"The en-suite vanity unit is leaking under the sink. Can you please fix it?" she texted.

"I will look at it when the flooring arrives," came the response.

Several days later, he returned to complete the flooring and address the leak.

"I have finished. I want to be paid today," he said.

"You haven't supplied me with any invoices or removed the rubbish. I have quotations but not invoices. I need the invoices for my records, so please provide them for all the work you have done here."

"I will send them over later," he sniffed and walked out, leaving the rubbish behind.

The invoices never arrived. When she opened the wardrobe door, she noticed that he had installed a random double socket halfway up the bedroom wall, which he had plugged the TV into. The Karndean flooring was fitted poorly and creaked every time she walked across it.

Her instincts were telling her that something was wrong. She had a knack for sensing trouble, and something didn't feel right about this man or his wife.

Sammy contacted an electrician because she needed an electrical report to sell or rent her apartment. He arrived promptly later that week to deliver the report. Unfortunately, the work that Sleazy had completed was inadequate.

"Who did the work? You should report him. Clearly, he is not qualified," Lee, from LRO Electrical said, shaking his head.

"LMG Design Ltd," she replied.

"He failed to install grommets in the new sockets, Sam. That makes it dangerous; he should not be doing electrical work if he isn't qualified. All the sockets he installed in your lounge, office, and bedroom have failed, and he tampered with an existing socket, which he should not have done," Lee explained.

Sammy was furious.

"I can fix this for you. Would you like a quote?" he offered.

"Yes, please, Lee. Thank you so much," she responded with a frown.

Lee was set to become her future electrician; he was trustworthy, professional, and qualified—exactly what she needed.

Sleazy then sent her a text:

"I am still waiting for payment," Sammy ignored him.

Later that evening, she was jolted from her thoughts by a series of sharp, insistent knocks at the door. Heart racing, she tiptoed across the dimly lit room, her breath catching in her throat. Peering through the spy-hole, she caught sight of him on the other side. He stood there, his face flushed with anger, his jaw set tight, the shadows amplifying the fury etched across his features.

She did not open it.

Chapter 20

Dean Owen,
No Duff U.K.
CIC

Since the founding of No Duff U.K., Dean Owen has been a cornerstone in nurturing the organisation's success, guiding its mission with unwavering determination and compassion. His remarkable skill set, fervent passion, and deeply personal experiences have ignited a spark of hope in many, empowering individuals to face their mental health battles head-on while courageously challenging the stigma that often surrounds these issues.

Dean's diverse background spans the HM Forces, HMP, Merseyside Police, and the RSPCA, where he has encountered a vast array of experiences that few can fathom. This rich tapestry of his life has forged a resilience in him, rendering him largely unfazed by the chaos and challenges he has witnessed. A heartfelt mission drives him: to extend a helping hand to those who, like him, have confronted the monsters lurking on the front lines yet continue to wrestle with their own inner demons and the pervasive shadows of mental illness.

Having retired from the Police Service in 2009, Dean's journey is not merely one of survival but of profound purpose, as he channels his energy into supporting others in their quests for healing and understanding.

Sammy reached out to Dean on LinkedIn, her message infused with a hopeful curiosity about whether he was in need of a counsellor.

From the moment they connected, their conversation flowed effortlessly, as they shared insights about the pandemic's profound impact on society and the cascading effects felt by first responders bravely serving on the front lines.

"I would welcome you on board with open arms, lovely. Are you BACP-registered?" Dean asked, his tone warm and inviting.

"Yes, I'm not only registered but also insured and fully equipped to work remotely," Sammy replied, a sense of pride in her voice.

"Fantastic! I have a contract with Merseyside Police, as their occupational health services are virtually non-existent at the moment," Dean shared, his enthusiasm unmistakable.

"I'm thrilled to hear that, thank you!" Sammy responded, a wave of gratitude washing over her.

True to his word, Dean swiftly forwarded the relevant vetting documentation, ensuring Sammy could begin her work without delay.

On September 16th, No Duff U.K. sent over a treasure trove of client details, and by the end of that month, Sammy had successfully secured nine clients from them. These clients included a diverse mix of valiant male and female officers, alongside dedicated administrative staff, all serving at Merseyside Police.

As October rolled in, Dean further bolstered her roster by sending her thirteen more clients. November brought five additional clients, and by December, two more joined her growing list. Each new connection added to Sammy's sense of purpose, equipping her to make a meaningful difference in the lives of those who risked their own for the safety of others.

She felt a deep sense of joy in her work, seeing as she regularly guided up to seven clients each day. While the pace was demanding and left her feeling depleted at times, it was a challenge she embraced wholeheartedly, as she truly believed her clients were remarkable individuals with inspiring stories and experiences. Meanwhile, Dean and Sammy often engaged in in-depth discussions about effective counselling techniques tailored specifically for law enforcement officers and veterans. They exchanged insights on the unique challenges these groups face, striving to develop best practices that would foster healing and resilience in their clients.

Chapter 21

No Good Deed Goes Unpunished

In mid-November, a chill hung in the air as Sammy received an unsettling notification from the Bournemouth Small Claims Court, informing her that LMG Design Ltd had filed a claim against her. The weight of the document felt heavy in her hands, a stark reminder of the conflict that lay ahead.

Determined to fight back, she diligently prepared her counterclaim, meticulously detailing the shoddy workmanship that Sleazy had inflicted upon her home. His electrical work, once hoped to illuminate her space, had instead plunged it into darkness, failing spectacularly. Sammy remembered the sting of having paid 75% of his quoted price, a payment that now felt like a bitter betrayal.

She crafted her counterclaim to not only address the faulty work but also to narrate the backstory of how she had crossed paths with Debbie Downer and Sleazy. She recounted their gradual descent into despair, worsened by the heavy toll of COVID-19 and its accompanying financial strain. In her attempt to assist a neighbour battling suicidal thoughts and a husband grappling with depression, she had unwittingly stepped into a web of deceit woven by those she sought to help. They had manipulated her goodwill and trust regarding Sleazy's skills, extracting money under false pretences. As she reflected on her experience, a sense of injustice washed over her. "No good deed goes unpunished," she silently mused.

Suddenly, her legal mind sprang to life, sparking a realisation: this could be a case of "obtaining money by deception," the thought churned in her stomach like a storm, fuelling her disdain for those who deceived others. Under the Fraud Act 2006, obtaining money by deception is a serious crime, and she knew the penalties could vary dramatically depending on the specific circumstances and the amount of money involved. Sammy felt a surge of determination; she was ready to seek justice.

She persevered in her work with Merseyside Police, deeply moved by the incredible strength and resilience exhibited by the officers and police staff she counselled. Their unwavering determination in the face of adversity inspired her.

The world felt as though it had spiralled into chaos. Anxiety hung heavy in the air, mental illness affected many, and the alarming rise in the suicide rate cast a shadow over society.

When a complex society collapses, it signifies a loss of cultural identity, social structure, and government, often leading to increased violence and disorder. Key features of societal collapse include the breakdown of law and order, population decline, and the loss of written records and monumental structures. Environmental degradation, disease, and economic instability can also contribute to this collapse.

Without a functioning government, legal systems, and law enforcement, society becomes increasingly vulnerable to crime, violence, and anarchy. Shared values, beliefs, and cultural practices may weaken or vanish, resulting in a decline in collective meaning and identity.

Population decline can accompany collapse due to factors such as conflict, famine, or disease. Trade routes, markets, and resource management systems may break down, causing shortages and economic hardship. Overexploitation of resources, deforestation, and pollution can further exacerbate societal issues and contribute to environmental collapse. As the pillars of governance and the rich tapestry of cultural identity crumble, invaluable written records, majestic monumental structures, and other signs of a once-complex society may fade into oblivion. In this unraveling of social order, turmoil reigns, as violence and conflict erupt frequently among individuals and groups in desperate competition for resources.

The fragile threads of social bonds fray, and the foundation of mutual trust erodes like sand slipping through fingers. In this chaotic landscape, unusual cults and alternative lifestyles begin to take root, offering a sense of belonging in an uncertain world. As the vast frameworks of society disintegrate, people often retreat into smaller, self-sufficient communities, seeking safety and stability in the face of adversity.

Amid this period of upheaval, the environment and the resilient human spirit may generate a spark of regeneration, eventually giving rise to fresh societal structures that reflect the lessons learned from the past and the desire for renewal.

Her clients at Merseyside Police were grappling with the harsh realities of COVID-19, which brought forth a troubling wave of human behaviour. They faced aggressive encounters—being spat at, assaulted, and verbally abused. Yet, each day, they donned their uniforms with unwavering courage, returning to the front lines like true heroes.

These brave officers were not just fighting external battles; they were also enduring personal tragedies. They were mourning the loss of family members, unable to find solace at funerals, and facing the weight of illnesses around them. Concerns about their own children, financial stresses, and an escalating mental health crisis loomed heavily on their shoulders. Despite these overwhelming challenges, they pressed on, keeping society safe while embodying the spirit of resilience—calmly carrying on in the face of adversity.

Inside the bustling control centre, the call handlers were met with a relentless storm of abuse and mounting hysteria, yet they stood firm, doing their best to respond with compassion and professionalism.

Sammy was in awe of these extraordinary individuals. She cherished every moment spent working alongside them, offering a safe haven where they could unwind—a space to talk candidly and release the burdens of their stress. In her presence, they found a glimmer of relief amid the chaos, reminding them they were not alone in their fight.

In the crisp air of early December, Sammy walked with purpose towards the bin store tucked away in the dimly lit underground car park. As she made her way, Stewart, the sardonic director of DFSB Ltd, brushed past her, his demeanour brimming with mockery.

"Morning!" he called out, a smirk playing on his lips.

"Don't talk to me," she shot back, her voice as cold as ice.

His laughter echoed through the confines of the car park. "Yeah, right... M O R N I N G!!!" he mocked, the aggression in his tone palpable.

Ignoring the tension, Sammy deposited her rubbish in the bin, then pulled out her iPhone. With a steady hand, she hit record and trailed after him as he approached a sleek black Range Rover parked nearby—a vehicle that didn't belong to him but to a resident of the building.

"I am talking to you, Stewart, and recording you," she said, her tone firm and unwavering. "I just told you not to talk to me, yet you ignored my request. So let me make myself crystal clear: do not engage with me again. Confirm that you understand and will comply," her eyes narrowed like a predator about to pounce.

As he slipped inside the car, attempting to close the door, she positioned herself firmly between him and his escape. With her iPhone raised like a shield, she refused to budge. When he tried to push her aside, she stood resolute, adopting a police stance and using her elbow to press against his throat.

"Now you've heard me loud and clear: leave me alone," she growled, her voice low and menacing.

Stepping aside, she allowed him to pull out of the space—but not without a flair. Just as he began to drive off, he rolled down the window, retrieved his phone, and dialled the concierge office, his tone dripping with challenges.

"Make sure the cameras are on," he instructed, a gleam of mischief in his eye.

With a childlike grin spreading across his face, he waved slowly at her as she exited the car park, a stark contrast to the tension that lingered just moments before.

Not long after, her phone rang, the caller ID flashing "Dorset Police," a wave of anger washed over her as she realised he had lodged a complaint of assault against her. With determination, she requested to speak with an inspector. As she recounted the series of events that led to this moment, her voice steady and firm, she made it clear that she was simply defending herself. After considering her explanation, the Dorset Police chose not to pursue the matter further.

Finally, she inquired with the inspector, "Did they provide you with any CCTV footage regarding the incident?"

"Yes," he replied, a note of professionalism in his voice.

She leaned forward slightly, a knowing glint in her eyes.

"Funny, isn't it, Sir? I've been asking for that very
CCTV footage, but each time I do, it seems the
cameras are mysteriously 'not working.'"

Later that week, Sammy received an unexpected
call from Gary, her contact at Phoenix. His tone
was serious as he began, "I've received a formal
complaint against you."

Sammy raised an eyebrow, intrigued. "What,
from one of your veterans?" she asked, the hint of
disbelief evident in her voice.

"No, it's actually from a civilian. She's not affiliated
with us at all," Gary clarified.

Curious about the situation, Sammy listened
intently as Gary explained the outline of the
complaint. Clearly it had come from Debbie Downer,
who had made some pointed accusations.

Sammy couldn't help but laugh at the absurdity of it
all.

"Ah," she chuckled, finding humour in the dramatic
nature of the complaint.

Gary continued, "I asked her for the name of the
client she alleges you breached confidentiality
with," he paused before adding, "But she couldn't
provide me with any details."

In late December, Sammy received an official notice
from the British Association for Counselling and

Psychotherapy (BACP) indicating that DFSB Ltd had filed a complaint against her. They accused her of exhibiting aggressive behaviour that allegedly disturbed them and upset fellow residents within their community.

In response, the BACP clarified to DFSB Ltd that they were not in a position to address the concerns raised in the complaint because DFSB Ltd was not a client of hers. This exchange left Sammy feeling exasperated with what she perceived as immature and unprofessional conduct from DFSB Ltd.

Determined to stand up for herself, Sammy decided to take further action. She composed a formal letter to the Information Commissioners Office, detailing her grievances and formally lodging a complaint against DFSB Ltd. In her letter, she outlined the situation, emphasising how their unfounded allegations had affected her reputation and well-being.

Dear Sir,

I am writing to provide details regarding my Subject Access Request email dated 18th December, which I sent to the concierge services at my residence. They have consistently ignored every email and letter I have sent them.

My relationship with them has been difficult since January 2021, when a member of their team inappropriately attempted to hug me.

This incident was not only extremely upsetting, but it also occurred during lockdown when personal protective equipment (PPE) was a legal requirement, and none of their employees were wearing it. I reported this matter, along with concerns about the fire marshal, to the police.

Since then, I have faced anger and hostility from the concierge staff. Any attempts to file a complaint, request the CCTV footage, or inquire about their complaints process have been ignored.

The services they provided regarding parcel deliveries were significantly reduced, leading me to feel victimised and discriminated against. Within days, my personal information was circulated throughout the complex, resulting in harassment from three staff members. The situation escalated to the point where I had to contact the police again and invest in a doorbell camera and a body-worn camera.

I am writing to express my concerns about the unprofessional conduct within the company. I have observed employees gossiping about residents in an unfavourable manner, not only to other residents but also to contractors and visitors. As I pay for this service, I am shocked by their level of indiscretion regarding the privacy of residents.

Additionally, I have experienced several alarming incidents where I was followed around the car park. When I requested the CCTV footage from

those specific dates, PMB Property Management
informed me that the cameras were not functioning
at that time.

If you need any further information, please do not
hesitate to contact me.

Yours sincerely,

She then wrote to the Information Commissioner's
Office regarding LMG Design Ltd.

Dear Sir,

LMG Design Ltd carried out approximately £7,000
worth of work on my property during 2020-2021.
The director performed electrical work that failed
inspection, and there is an upcoming civil court
case at Bournemouth Court related to this issue.
He did not have the necessary qualifications to
carry out electrical work, which jeopardised my
property's safety.

After I submitted my counterclaim in November
2021, the director shared it with his wife. They
subsequently engaged in a course of conduct that
involved harassment and slander by submitting
a written complaint against me to my client,
Phoenix Heroes. Additionally, they informed other
residents and contractors in my area that "I don't
pay my bills," as a result, I have been subjected
to scorn from their acquaintances in local shops,
and I received disdainful looks from a resident I

don't know while disposing of my rubbish in the bin store.

LMG Design Ltd had no right to disclose details of our civil dispute to others. Their actions have caused me significant distress and have resulted in me being victimised by DFSB Ltd and HCS Cleaning Services Ltd, who work regularly at my residence.

For context, all the companies mentioned above have previously provided various goods and services to my residential complex. I would like to point out that LMG Design Ltd is also my neighbour, which adds another layer of complexity to this situation.

Unfortunately, DFSB Ltd has been engaging in a pattern of behaviour that I can only describe as bullying, harassment, slander, and discrimination. They went so far as to report me to my regulatory body, alleging that I was rude and aggressive toward their staff and other residents. I would like to clarify that this complaint was not pursued further, as DFSB Ltd is not a client of mine.

In an even more concerning turn of events, they have also contacted the police regarding me. Additionally, a director of DFSB Ltd has been following me around our complex and taking photographs of my front door. I find this behaviour incredibly unsettling and have no idea why a director of the company would take photos of my residence. For your review, I have included the video footage captured by my doorbell camera as evidence of their actions.

HCS Cleaning Services Ltd is the on-site cleaning contractor that also provides private window cleaning for my apartment. I have paid them for their services on several occasions. However, they recently refused to clean my property, claiming they were informed that "I don't pay my bills," this misleading information was shared by LMG Design Ltd and is both untrue and defamatory. It is worth noting that all three directors of these companies are friends.

The civil court case between myself and LMG Design Ltd is a private matter that should not have been discussed with others. I am not a debtor and do not owe any money to these companies.

Furthermore, LMG Design Ltd has been sharing private and confidential business information with others, including DFSB Ltd and HCS Cleaning Services Ltd, regarding my personal matters. I believe they are colluding and sharing information that should be protected under GDPR. This behaviour is unacceptable.

Since July 2021, I have been requesting information from LMG Design Ltd under a Subject Access Request (SAR). Specifically, I am seeking invoices related to the work they performed at my residence, along with any emails and texts exchanged between us, as well as payment receipts. Their refusal to provide this information raises concerns about their business practices.

If you require any further information, please do not hesitate to contact me.

Yours sincerely,

Sammy penned a letter to HCS Cleaning Services Ltd, expressing her frustration after hearing from a neighbour and friend that they had spread rumours about her not paying her bills. With determination, she requested copies of every invoice issued to her since 2013, along with any outstanding amounts still owed.

Despite the seriousness of her inquiry, all she received in return was silence. Yet, the moment she crossed paths with Michael in the dimly lit car park, she felt his piercing gaze and the dismissive sniff that escaped him, a subtle but clear indication of disdain.

A few days later, she encountered yet another unwelcome surprise. The access she had enjoyed for nine years—using her door fob to reach the lift connected to Debbie Downer's door—had vanished. This privilege had been her lifeline for transporting large parcels, so its abrupt removal felt like a calculated blow. The action was orchestrated by DFSB Ltd, the company that controlled the access from their office, leaving Sammy astonished.

Chapter 22

Storm Arwen & South Yorkshire Police Suicide Conference

Nick Knowles, the passionate Suicide Lead for South Yorkshire Police, reached out to her through LinkedIn with an exciting opportunity. He invited her to deliver a keynote presentation at the iconic Sheffield United Football Stadium, where she would address not just South Yorkshire Police officers but also high-ranking officials from police departments across the nation.

Filled with enthusiasm, she gladly accepted the invitation and set to work crafting her keynote address. She felt a sense of urgency to convey critical statistics: that one in five police officers grapples with PTSD, and that an alarming average of 23 officers tragically lose their lives to suicide each year. These were vital messages she believed needed to resonate with the senior management.

Her keynote was designed to last an hour, during which she envisioned a dynamic blend of striking images, compelling videos, and poignant research statistics that would captivate her audience.

Nick shared the exciting news that the Metropolitan Police Commissioner would be in attendance, alongside the Chief Constable of South Yorkshire Police. These high-profile figures needed to hear this information, as it was crucial for them to cascade these important insights down through their ranks.

The day before the event, she booked a hotel nestled in South Yorkshire, just a stone's throw from the stadium, and embarked on a four-hour drive filled with anticipation and nerves.

The next morning, she rose early, the sun casting a golden hue through her hotel window. She sipped a few too many cups of strong coffee, feeling the familiar buzz of adrenaline, as she made her way to the stadium, where Nick awaited her with a warm welcome.

"It's wonderful to have you here, Sam," he said with genuine enthusiasm, his eyes sparkling with excitement. "You're really making a name for yourself, and I can't wait to hear your keynote!"

"Thank you," she replied, feeling a swell of pride at his encouraging words.

The conference unfolded smoothly, her keynote delivery captivating the audience despite a few initial technical hiccups. She had crafted an engaging knowledge check for the end of her presentation, relishing the opportunity to see who had truly absorbed her insights. To make the event even more memorable, she brought along enticing prizes: a beautiful globe on a stand for the top prize, a mesmerising Newton's Cradle for second place, and a signed copy of her debut book, "Suicidal State," for third.

It was no surprise when the Chief Constable claimed first prize, adding a touch of light-heartedness to the serious nature of the day.

After the conference, she was eager to reconnect with Andy "Otis" Reading, a steadfast companion from her days on the police force. Their bond stretched back 33 years, and he was more than just a colleague—he was like an older brother who had always been there for her. In moments of trouble, fear, or distress, he stood by her side, a comforting presence in a chaotic world. Alongside him was his wonderful wife, Linda, whose warmth and kindness made their home feel like a sanctuary.

As she battled through the evening traffic, the city's lights blurred past her like streaks of stars. When she finally reached his home, the fatigue of the day melted away as she wrapped him in a tight embrace. She could feel the weight of exhaustion in her bones.

"You look knackered," he observed, his eyes twinkling with concern.

"I am," she admitted, a weary smile tugging at her lips.

In the cosy kitchen, Linda was busy preparing homemade chips, their enticing aroma wafting through the air. The heart of their home, the kitchen, buzzed with laughter and stories as they reminisced about the past. Otis's house was a beautiful reflection of his personal touch—immaculate, well-presented, and filled with cherished memories that spoke of years of hard work.

Dinner was a feast, and she savoured every bite of the delicious meal, her heart swelling with gratitude. As the evening wore on, a deeper weariness settled in.

"Mind if I turn in early, Otis? I'm shattered, and I have a long drive tomorrow. I'll be up and gone before you wake," she said, stifling a yawn that threatened to reveal just how tired she truly felt.

"Of course! Just help yourself to tea and coffee when you wake up," Otis replied with a warm smile.

"Thanks, mate. Thank you, Linda. Goodnight," she said, her voice heavy with sleep.

As the night deepened, Sammy's sleep was restless, her mind dancing between wakefulness and dreams. At 5am, she finally stirred, the early morning light gently filtering through the window. After two steaming cups of tea invigorated her, she braced herself for the journey home, only to find herself facing the fierce winds and rain of Storm Arwen that roared outside, ready to test her resolve as she hit the road.

Storm Arwen was a formidable extratropical cyclone that unleashed its fury during the 2021-22 European windstorm season. This tempest swept across the United Kingdom, Ireland, and France, bringing with it fierce winds and swirling snow that transformed landscapes into a winter wonderland gone wild. Tragically, the storm claimed at least three lives and left countless homes without power, as its relentless gales battered communities. The damage was intensified by the unusual northerly winds that howled with an extraordinary ferocity.

On 25th November 2021, the Met Office officially named Storm Arwen, signalling the severity of the approaching chaos. Red wind warnings were sounded for the northeastern regions of the UK, while extensive amber and yellow warnings blanketed much of Scotland, Northern Ireland, Wales, and England. The roaring seas generated hazardous waves that disrupted ferry services, casting a veil of uncertainty over maritime travel.

As the clock struck 5pm on 26th November,
Network Rail made the critical decision to close
rail lines north of Berwick-upon-Tweed, while
LNER suspended train services north of Newcastle,
leaving many stranded. In Greater Manchester,
over 120 lorries became trapped in a thick snowy
embrace on the M62, leading police to shut down
the motorway as snowploughs and gritters
ventured out on rescue missions amidst the storm's
fury. The Tyne and Wear Metro network, in a
rare gesture of understatement, declared, "This
is the worst winter storm to hit the Metro in 41
years of operations," highlighting the severity of
the conditions that paralysed one of the region's
lifelines.

The UK Met Office sounded an alarm with a rare
red weather warning, as a powerful deep pressure
system swept southward from the turbulent
Atlantic Ocean. This ominous forecast predicted
ferocious winds and gigantic waves crashing
along the eastern coastline of Scotland, from
the rugged shores of Aberdeenshire all the way
down to the Tees Estuary in England. Red wind
warnings painted the northeastern UK in a stark
hue of caution, while extensive amber and yellow
warnings blanketed much of Scotland, Northern
Ireland, Wales, and a vast swath of England. The
terrifying prospect of monstrous waves loomed,
threatening to disrupt ferry services and maroon
travellers.

The storm's destructive force was intensified by relentless winds, howling at over 90 mph, and, unusually, sweeping in from the northeast. This unexpected direction battered trees that had never faced such fierce gusts, leaving them vulnerable and uprooted.

In the wake of the storm, a staggering 112,000 homes in northern England were plunged into darkness, while 80,000 households in Scotland found themselves without power, and 13,000 homes in Wales felt the bitter bite of the outages too.

By 30th November, a persistent 45,000 consumers across the UK remained without electricity, as reported by the Energy Networks Association (ENA). In response to the widespread chaos caused, network operators faced the daunting task of compensating the affected, with a hefty bill totalling £44 million looming over them.

Countless individuals found themselves plunged into darkness for an entire week, depending on local shops and cafes for essential sustenance and comforts. Northern Powergrid announced that Arwen was the most ferocious storm to batter their network since 2005, necessitating extensive repairs as vast stretches of overhead power lines lay in ruins. Despite the tireless efforts of restoration teams, thousands of homes remained in darkness, with power only fully restored on 7th December.

The storm wreaked havoc on the natural landscape, leaving an estimated eight million trees in Scotland battered or uprooted. The enduring aftermath signals that many of the region's lush forests will take decades to regenerate to their former splendour.

Across the UK, police agencies reported a distressing number of accidents, as roadways were rendered impassable by fallen trees, treacherous snow, and icy patches. On the M62 in Greater Manchester, more than 120 lorries became trapped in the relentless snow, prompting police to shut down the motorway while snowploughs and gritters valiantly worked to free them.

In a heartbreaking twist of fate, a man in the Northern Irish town of Antrim tragically lost his life when a massive tree crashed down onto his car. Another individual in Cumbria met a similar fate, fatally struck by a falling tree, while a third man in Aberdeenshire perished when a tree collided violently with his pickup truck.

The storm unleashed winds howling at up to 100 miles per hour, stirring up monstrous waves along the Scottish coast that soared to heights exceeding 33 feet, a spectacular yet terrifying display of nature's raw power.

Sammy's heart raced as the relentless rain transformed the motorway into a slick, shimmering expanse. Each drop blurred her vision, making the white lines that divided the lanes appear like ghostly shadows. Just when she thought it couldn't get worse, the raindrops morphed into swirling snowflakes, dancing wildly in the air before settling on the asphalt. Panic gripped her, tightening her body as if encased in ice.

The massive lorries around her began to slow, their hazard lights flickering like warning beacons in the storm. With a determined breath, she manoeuvred into the left-hand lane, easing her speed down to 50 mph, then further to 30 mph, her hands clenched tightly around the steering wheel. The task of keeping her car on the road felt like navigating a treacherous slide, with visibility reduced to mere shadows. But stopping was not an option; she understood that remaining in motion was her best defence against the chaos surrounding her.

After what felt like an eternity, Sammy finally pulled into her driveway, drained and depleted. The journey that should have taken a couple of hours had turned into a gruelling seven. Her neck throbbed painfully, and every muscle in her body ached, leaving her feeling as stiff as a board, but relief washed over her as she stepped into the warmth of home.

Pawsey, with her piercing green eyes, looked less than impressed. She fixed Sammy with that unmistakable feline gaze, the kind that only cat owners can interpret—it seemed to say, "And just where have you been all this time?"

Overwhelmed with a sense of relief and joy at home, Sammy scooped Pawsey into her arms and enveloped her in a warm, comforting embrace. The soft purring that emerged from the little cat was music to her ears. After showering her beloved pet with affection, she set out to make sure Pawsey was well taken care of, filling her bowl with enticing Likelix, refreshing her water, and meticulously emptying, cleaning, and refreshing her litter tray.

Feeling the stress of the day melt away, Sammy decided it was time to pamper herself. She ran a luxurious bath, pouring in generous amounts of Radox muscle relief, the sweet scent of lavender and eucalyptus wafting through the air. Dipping her toes into the warm water, she grabbed her phone to text her masseuse, relief flooding her at the thought of some much-needed relaxation.

Luckily, her masseuse replied quickly, confirming availability for the next day, which brought a smile to Sammy's face.

Once she finished her blissful soak, Sammy slipped into her fleece pyjamas, the plush fabric wrapping her in warmth and comfort. With a contented sigh, she crawled into bed, her eyelids growing heavier with each passing moment. Within moments, she drifted off to sleep, utterly at peace.

CHAPTER 23

Griffeye & The National Crime Agency

In the crisp air of early December, she made her way to Tower Bridge Hotel in London, a striking edifice that elegantly spanned the River Thames. The occasion was a pivotal conference where she would present to an assembly of dedicated professionals from the National Crime Agency, Metropolitan Police, Kent Police, and various other law enforcement agencies, all focused on the grim realities of Online Child Sexual Abuse. This important event had been orchestrated by Griffeye Technologies, a trailblazer in developing sophisticated technology designed to compile images of child pornography for use as critical evidence in legal proceedings.

In the daunting world of child exploitation investigations, the stakes were high; to advance a case with the Crown Prosecution Service, detectives were mandated to gather at least 100 images—a threshold that haunted their every step. Consequently, these tireless officers found themselves sifting through countless harrowing images, each one a painful reminder of the abhorrent realities they fought against.

The nature of their work was undeniably distressing, with the toll it took on their mental health manifesting as symptoms of PTSD in many who faced such haunting evidence day in and day out.

With this in mind, she meticulously designed her Keynote presentation, pouring her heart into creating a resource that would resonate deeply with the detectives, offering them both insight and support as they navigated their challenging work.

Child Sexual Exploitation (CSE) is a specific form of CSA. It occurs when an individual or group exploits an imbalance of power to coerce, manipulate, or deceive a child or young person under the age of 18 into sexual activities. This exploitation may occur (a) in exchange for something the victim needs or desires, and/or (b) for the financial gain or increased status of the perpetrator or facilitator. Even if the activity appears consensual, the victim can still be considered as having been sexually exploited.

Online CSA and CSE offences can take various forms, including:

- **Online Grooming**: This refers to developing a relationship with a child to enable their abuse and exploitation, both online and offline. Online platforms such as social media, messaging apps, and live streaming can be used to facilitate this type of offending.

Live Streaming: Live streaming services can be exploited by Child Sex Offenders (CSOs) to encourage victims to engage in or observe sexual acts via webcam. CSOs may also stream or view live instances of contact sexual abuse or indecent images of children, often in collaboration with other offenders. In some cases, CSOs will pay facilitators to stream live contact abuse, directing what sexual acts are perpetrated against the victim.

A child is defined as anyone under the age of 18. Child Sexual Abuse (CSA) involves forcing or enticing a child to participate in sexual activities, regardless of whether the child is aware of what is occurring. This may include actions such as involving children in viewing or producing sexual images, observing sexual activities, encouraging children to engage in sexually inappropriate behaviours, or grooming a child in preparation for abuse.

In the conference room, a sea of approximately 30 officers sat, their faces etched with the shadows of trauma. The atmosphere was heavy with unspoken hurt as Sammy stepped forward to open her keynote. Dressed in her Phoenix Heroes hoodie, she commanded attention, her presence a blend of strength and vulnerability.

As she introduced herself, she unfolded her story — a journey that began in the ranks of the Royal Military Police, followed by her challenging tenure with the West Midlands Police. Her voice trembled slightly as she recounted the devastating loss of her brother to suicide, a wound that had shaped her path. With heartfelt sincerity, she described her work as a counsellor, supporting fellow veterans through organisations like Phoenix Heroes CIC and No Duff U.K., as well as offering her services to private individuals struggling with their own demons.

The officers leaned forward, their gazes fixed on her, captivated by the raw honesty in her words. Sammy illuminated the complexities of PTSD, skilfully revealing the alarming realities that many police officers face — the haunting spectre of mental health struggles that can lead to suicidal thoughts and, tragically, to loss of life. Her message resonated deeply, igniting a spark of awareness and understanding in the room as they absorbed the weight of her insights and experiences.

"My colleague took his own life last week; he was part of my unit," the sergeant revealed, his voice heavy with sorrow.

"And how are you coping with that?" she inquired gently, her eyes full of concern.

"Numb," he replied, the word hanging in the air like a heavy fog.

"How do you manage to deal with the haunting images you witness?" Sammy pressed, her curiosity mingling with empathy.

"I dissociate," he stated flatly, a glimpse of the emotional armour he donned to shield himself from the haunting realities of his work.

"I think you are incredibly brave to engage in this line of work; it's extraordinarily dark. Thank you for your unwavering service," she expressed, her tone laced with admiration.

"Someone has to do it. Eventually, you just learn to normalise it," he answered, a flicker of resignation in his eyes. "The technology that Griffeye has developed has been a game changer for us; it significantly reduces the number of images we have to confront. It can recognise body parts of children, as well as familiar backgrounds like curtains, beds, and artwork," he gestured as if trying to brush away the weight of his words.

"That's truly amazing," she remarked, her voice a mix of awe and disbelief as she absorbed the gravity of his reality.

"I'm deeply worried that many of my officers are not receiving the mental health support they rightfully need," the sergeant said, his brow furrowed with concern. "Would you be able to come to our department and provide some training on PTSD?"

"Absolutely, I'll share my contact details with you afterwards. Thank you for reaching out," Samantha responded, her voice warm with understanding.

As the clock struck 4pm, the presentation wrapped up, leaving Samantha with a sense of fulfilment. She stepped outside into the dusky embrace of central London, the city's lights flickering to life around her. However, her moment of pride quickly turned to annoyance as the unmistakable flash of a speed camera lit up her rearview mirror. She realised with a sinking feeling that she had been speeding—her car had been gliding at 30 mph in a 20 mph zone, the thrill of the moment now overshadowed by the impending consequences.

CHAPTER 24

El Chapo of Merseyside Police

On 16th December, she met via telephone "El Chapo" of Merseyside Police. He had served in the Royal Engineers, Cheshire Police and Merseyside Police. It was evident that he was highly professional, highly educated, and highly skilled. It was further evident that he was highly pissed off.

The term "Royal Engineer" refers to a member of the Corps of Royal Engineers within the British Army. These soldiers, commonly known as Sappers, are multi-skilled and provide essential engineering and technical support across all areas of the army, both in peacetime and during operations. The Royal Engineers offer a wide range of services, including combat engineering, infrastructure development, and disaster relief.

They undergo specialised training in various engineering disciplines, equipping them to handle diverse tasks in different environments.

The Corps of Royal Engineers has a long and distinguished history that dates back to 1717. They have participated in numerous military campaigns and operations. Royal Engineers are skilled in various trades and specialities, including construction, maintenance, demolition, and communication. The Corps is organised into different wings and branches, each specialising in specific aspects of military engineering.

Her client began to tell her the reason he wanted counselling. The Firearms Unit were undergoing refurbishment of their HQ. In the skip in the car park lay a "Big Red Key" or "Enforcer" as they are affectionately known. El Chapo, being a former Engineer of the Royal variety, could not let it go to waste.

He took the Enforcer out of a skip, placed it in the boot of his car, and brought it home to make a weight to weigh down an umbrella parasol.

In September, a police car activated its blue lights and stopped him at 7am on his first day back to work after paternity leave. He was arrested. He was shocked and felt crushed by the situation.

Merseyside Police, as part of their crackdown on serious and organised crime, arrested him for theft, despite the cost of the stolen property being only £1.75. The investigation that followed, however, cost hundreds of thousands of pounds. As a result, her client was suspended from work, but remained on full pay.

El Chapo stood tall, embodying pride in every aspect of his life. He revelled in his achievements, cherished his loving wife and children, and valued the strong relationships he had cultivated over the years. His dedication to his service in both the military and law enforcement added to his sense of identity. So when he found himself facing arrest for theft, it felt like the ground had been ripped from beneath him.

"They did what?" Sammy gasped, her eyes wide in disbelief as he recounted the shocking events.

"I can't believe it; I'm still in shock! They've suspended me," he said, frustration lacing his voice.

Sammy could feel the waves of anger and hurt emanating from him, and her own indignation surged in response to the absurdity of the allegation.

They delved into a detailed discussion about the Theft Act, dissecting every aspect until they both reached the same conclusion: there was no way he could have committed theft, especially since the property in question was sitting in a skip. The entire situation was utterly preposterous, and she couldn't shake the feeling that he was being targeted and set up.

The Professional Standards Department was delving into his affairs, and he felt utterly bewildered by the turn of events. His colleagues in the firearms unit shared his disbelief, their faces mirroring his shock.

"I can't wrap my head around why they're pursuing this," he said, voice low and incredulous. "I told them I have the enforcer—it's sitting right in my garden. I've got nothing to hide; I didn't steal it; it was just tossed in the skip! Now, they're alleging I sold police property, specifically issued boots. Truth is, I haven't sold their boots—no one wears them since they're practically useless. It was my own boots I sold on eBay. They've combed through my eBay account, my wife's account, even rifled through my phone. Jesus, Sam, I feel like I'm living in a crime drama! I'm still in shock."

"That's absolutely ludicrous," Sammy replied, shaking her head in disbelief. "They've got serious organised crime to tackle in Merseyside, and instead, they're squandering time and public resources investigating you for a few quid over stuff that was just thrown away. It's insane!"

Merseyside Police employs firearms officers, also known as authorised firearms officers (AFOs) and specialised firearms officers (SFOs). These officers are specially trained and accredited to handle firearms in support of various police operations.

AFOs are involved in a range of firearms-related activities, including responding to incidents, providing expert advice, and managing firearm licensing. They are the first responders to incidents involving firearms, ensuring public safety and delivering an initial investigative response. Additionally, they offer guidance on maximising evidential opportunities during investigations.

These officers are responsible for all firearm discharges and recoveries, ensuring that proper handling procedures are followed carefully, especially when it comes to the issuance, renewal, and modification of firearm certificates. This is crucial for ensuring public safety and compliance with relevant regulations.

The authorities are dedicated to promoting responsible firearm ownership and secure storage, addressing concerns related to misuse or unsafe practices. Their primary focus is on public safety, particularly in managing situations where firearms may be linked to mental health issues or other risks.

Firearm officers (AFOs) undergo rigorous training and are accredited to handle firearms, ensuring they are proficient and safe. They play a vital role in investigating firearm-related incidents, gathering evidence, and supporting the prosecution of offenders. Additionally, they collaborate with intelligence teams to identify and assess potential risks associated with firearms, including incidents of discharges and recoveries.

AFOs prioritise public safety in all their actions, ensuring that weapons are handled responsibly and risks are minimised. They are responsible for capturing and preserving evidence at firearm-related incidents, which contributes to successful investigations. Additionally, they work to ensure that investigations progress efficiently, ultimately bringing offenders to justice.

"God knows how long this investigation will drag on, and the price tag attached to it will be astronomical. It's such a colossal waste of money! I offered to shoulder the costs; I never intended to steal anything. If they want the money back, they can have it. On top of that, they've accused me of pilfering a saw blade from a store, which is downright absurd. I borrowed a saw blade from the store; I certainly didn't steal it. We're always using things when we're in stores.

And as if that weren't enough, I'm also under scrutiny for 'theft' of food from the canteen—a packet of Mug Shot noodles. They cost a mere 89p. Here's the punchline... they are given out free by occupational health!"

He looked at her, his eyes heavy with frustration.

"Are you kidding me?" she asked, disbelief etched on her face.

"I wish I could be, Sam. I really do," he said, his voice filled with sadness.

"How are you feeling about all of this?" she asked gently.

"Shocked, angry, and deeply disappointed," he responded, his voice steady but heavy with emotion.

"No Duff U.K." has authorised eight sessions for you with me. You can use these sessions to express what's on your mind, and I'll help you navigate your anger and improve your well-being. How does that sound?" she inquired, her tone warm and reassuring.

"Great! I've heard so much about you. While my experience with the Merseyside Occupational Health counsellors was disappointing, your outstanding reputation truly stands out.
It's refreshing to connect with someone who understands the intricacies of the job without being bound by it. Trust is essential, especially when it comes to confidentiality, and I believe we can build that together," he said.

"Thank you. I will keep our sessions confidential, and I won't be giving any information to your investigators; legally, I'm not required to," she assured him.

"Brilliant!" he replied excitedly.

"Shall we schedule the same time next week?" she asked.

"Yeah, that sounds great," he responded.

"You will receive an email confirming your appointment. We'll speak next week, and look out for an email with information on anger management psychoeducation as well," she told him.

"Okay, see you!" he said.

As soon as the call ended, Sammy made her way to the kitchen, urgency in her steps. The kettle hissed to life as she filled it with water, her mind swirling with disbelief over the absurdity of the situation—what a farce it had all been. Each moment replayed in her mind like a scene from a poorly written drama. The following week, the phone rang, and her client's name appeared on the screen, pulling her out of her thoughts.

"They've now served me with a notice, saying I've breached police regulations because I sent some images on my phone that they consider inappropriate," he said, frustration evident in his tone.

"What kind of images were they?" Sammy asked, her curiosity piqued.

"Just the usual, really—a screen grab taken from Thorpe Park by the Detonator ride that got passed around," he explained, rolling his eyes at the absurdity of it all.

"Oh, so this is serious enough for criminal proceedings and misconduct?" she pressed, her brows furrowing with concern.

"Yeah," he said, resignation creeping into his voice.

"Are you getting support from The Federation?" she questioned, her expression softening.

"Yes, and my representative is solid; he finds the whole situation laughable, too. There's no way I've committed theft, especially since the value of the goods falls below the prosecution threshold. I know exactly who's played me—the snake who's twisted the knife in my back. He's been green with envy because I've held Bronze Commander roles and he hasn't. We've seen our share of chaos, including the Raoul Moat incident in 2010, along with countless other critical situations. After nineteen years on the job, it's disheartening to see how this pandemic has pushed people over the edge," he confided, a weary look washing over his face.

"I'm truly sorry you're having to endure this," she said softly, her eyes filled with concern. After a moment, she leaned in slightly and asked, "What do you think is causing all of this turmoil in your life?"

His face darkened with anger as he responded, "It's that snake who's jealous of me."

She shifted her posture, eager to understand his world better. "How has work been for you these days? Did the lockdowns affect you at all?"

He sighed deeply, running a hand across his head. "A mix of factors has been at play here. The Covid lockdowns, relentless policing efforts, and significant breakthroughs in combating organised crime have collectively contributed to a decrease in firearm-related incidents overall. Yet, I can't shake the feeling that the tide may be turning, especially with the early signs of change creeping in, particularly in Merseyside," he said, his expression clouded with concern as he spoke.

"Since 2015, gun offences had been on an unsettling rise throughout England and Wales, but then the pandemic swept in like a storm, turning life upside down. The harsh realities of lockdowns cast a long shadow over daily existence, leaving once-bustling streets eerily quiet and altering the very fabric of crime itself. With fewer people out and about, the patterns of criminal activity shifted dramatically, making it increasingly challenging for offenders to navigate through the desolate urban landscapes. In 2020, Merseyside Police reported 83 shooting incidents, but as the strict measures confined movements, this number dwindled, revealing a glimmer of hope amidst the chaos," he shared this information, his voice tinged with pride.

"You truly make a difference," she responded warmly.

"Thanks, Sam. You really should have submitted your application for a firearms license after your time in the Military Police. Was there a specific reason you didn't pursue that?" he inquired, curiosity evident in his tone.

"I chose a different path," she replied thoughtfully, a hint of nostalgia in her voice. "I always preferred the intricate work of a detective, unraveling mysteries rather than just focusing on the physical aspects of law enforcement."

"In 2021, Merseyside Police initiated a dynamic and specialised team aimed at countering the pressing threats posed by the twin scourges of drug trafficking and firearms violence. As desperation engulfed communities, law enforcement felt compelled to adopt bolder tactics in the face of escalating criminal activity. Contrary to the assertions of senior police officials who claim that obtaining a firearm in Britain poses significant challenges, the reality in Liverpool tells a different story. Here, a firearm can be procured for a mere £150, provided one knows where to inquire.

The connection between gun crime and drug distribution is well established, with drug gangs commanding the landscape of organised crime. At the pinnacle of this illicit hierarchy, these syndicates orchestrate the importation of narcotics destined for the UK market. The retail facet has become increasingly dominated by a new and ruthless business model known as County Lines Gangs. These networks communicate using specialised mobile phones that facilitate customer orders and the seamless relocation of drugs across the nation, all while heightening the risk of violent confrontations involving both firearms and knives.

Liverpool has emerged as a critical epicentre within the United Kingdom's complex and shadowy drug gang landscape. In the spring of 2020, a monumental shift occurred in the battle against organised crime when French law enforcement successfully breached the impregnable fortress of the Encrochat encrypted phone network. This cutting-edge technology had become an indispensable tool for criminals, particularly those in the drug trade, providing them with a seemingly unassailable means to craft and coordinate their sinister operations. He informed her.

"They've apprehended a lot of them now, thank goodness," Sammy remarked, relief evident in her tone.

"The dismantling of the Encrochat server in France enabled the police to access their messages within mere seconds of being sent. This unprecedented breakthrough led to over a thousand arrests across the UK. Many faced insurmountable evidence and chose to plead guilty. This crackdown coincided painfully with the onset of the coronavirus pandemic, which intensified the pressure on vile criminals, exacerbated by the constraints of lockdowns," he paused, the weight of the situation hanging heavily in the air.

"It's quite a whirlwind; I've been doing my best to avoid people as much as possible. Anyway, I wanted to share that I'll be taking a couple of weeks off over Christmas, so your next appointment will be in January," she said, her voice steady but tinged with a hint of excitement.

"Oh, of course! I completely understand," he replied, a curious glimmer in his eyes. "Do you have any fun plans for the holidays?" he added, leaning forward slightly.

"I'm preparing for a big adventure! I'll be moving to the sun-kissed shores of Barbados. I leave on 17th January for a whole year," she revealed, a smile spreading across her face as she envisioned the turquoise waters and balmy breezes.

"That's incredible! Will you be able to continue our sessions from there?" he queried, his interest piqued.

"Absolutely! We'll keep everything running smoothly as usual. I'll schedule our next session for the same time next week. Just keep an eye out for your psycho-education materials and the booking confirmation emails," she assured him, her confidence shining through.

As Sammy stepped into her kitchen to brew a steaming cup of tea, she allowed herself to reflect on the fascinating advancements in technology and their crucial role in fighting crime. A smile crossed her lips; it was remarkable how the pandemic had inadvertently led to a decrease in criminal activities—there truly was a silver lining amidst the chaos. Yet, a spark of confusion lingered in her mind. Why was her client being unfairly targeted? What hidden motives were driving this witch-hunt? It felt like an elaborate waste of precious time and taxpayer money, resources that could be better spent elsewhere.

The following week, her client opened up about his journey since their last session, a mixture of frustration and unexpected gratitude etched across his face.

"I'm getting accustomed to my suspension now. I'm trying to focus on the positives, just like you suggested. Spending time with my youngest daughter has been a blessing; I never imagined I'd enjoy being a house husband so much. My wife is truly appreciative; she works tirelessly, and I can see how much she values my support.

Merseyside has summoned my wife and her brother, her father and my best friend for questioning—they're convinced I've committed theft and even asked him if I sold him my old issue boots. Those boots are safely tucked away in my locker, but they refuse to acknowledge that fact.

The woman leading the investigation has proven to be particularly infuriating; her relentless agenda clouds her judgement, and her condescending tone only adds to my family's stress. I'm seething with anger," he confided, frustration spilling out like a shaken bottle of soda.

"Are you finding these sessions beneficial?" she inquired, her voice a soothing presence amid his turmoil.

"Absolutely," he replied sincerely.

He then shifted gears, the tension in his expression softening into a wry smile. "I referred to someone as a 'puff' in a private message on my phone. It's a term I've tossed around since my school days, during my time in the military, and throughout my police career. To me, it merely described someone lacking courage, never meant as a homophobic slur. The management in the police seem to forget that not all of us grew up in this modern LGBTQ era—my language is deeply ingrained from years of habit. I call a spade a spade, an Irishman 'Paddy', a Welshman 'Taff', a Scotsman 'Jock', and a twat a twat," he chuckled, the humour a brief reprieve from his frustrations.

It was enjoyable to hear her client laugh. Freud suggests that humour acts as a defence mechanism. Philosophers like Plato and Aristotle have attempted to explain humour since ancient times, and modern scholars have introduced various theories to elucidate its underlying mechanisms.

Martin and Ford (2018) outline the three main theories of humor. The first, relief theory, emphasises the motivational aspects related to interpersonal needs, arguing that humour provides relief from tension. They liken this to a hydraulic engine, where laughter functions as a pressure valve, releasing pent-up stress and anxiety.

More specifically, the physical processes of laughter—the muscular and respiratory activities—play a crucial role in releasing accumulated nervous energy (Martin & Ford, 2018).

The second theory introduced by Martin and Ford (2018) is superiority theory, which focuses on interpersonal motivations. This theory posits that humour arises from feelings of triumph over others' misfortunes or mistakes, thus enhancing one's self-esteem and promoting feelings of superiority.

The third theory, incongruity theory, examines the cognitive aspects of perception and interpretation. It suggests that humor is rooted in the perception of incongruity—when expectations do not align with reality (Martin & Ford, 2018). Laughter often results when the outcome is unexpected, as humor typically derives from surprise.

In fact, incongruity theory is considered the most influential of the humour theories. Many propose that "incongruity is at the core of all humour," this idea is intuitive: a joke with an obvious punchline fails to be funny. Instead, humour arises from unexpected punchlines or those that deviate from typical patterns.

"My friend Kian is gay, and we talked about words that offend him. He mentioned that he finds the term 'shirt-lifter' the most offensive. He then asked me what words offended me during my time in the police. I was called everything: filth, slag, slut, lezzer, pig, fascist, plod, Old Bill, rozzer, and fed. One time, while I was off duty and out with friends at the pub, a guy even made pig snorting noises behind me," Sammy disclosed.

"I know how that feels, but it's like water off a duck's back, isn't it? I've been called the same things, but not 'lezzer'!" El Chapo laughed.

"Sticks and stones may break my bones, but names will never hurt me. Was the person you referred to as a 'puff' informed that you had?" Sammy asked.

"Yes, he was, and he wasn't bothered by it," El Chapo replied. "He calls me much worse, and I'm not offended. The world has gone woke; it's full of namby pamby, wishy washy overly sensitive, childish, tree-hugging, sandal-wearing morons," he concluded.

"I agree, my learned friend, I agree," Sammy laughed, then asked, "What was the racist text?"

"It was an image that had been making the rounds on social media—a striking photo of a woman clad in a burkha, standing next to the towering Detonator ride at Thorpe Park," he revealed, a hint of nostalgia crossing his face.

"Oh, that one! Yes, someone sent it to me a while back. But just to clarify, you didn't create that image, did you? Did you add any comments when you forwarded it? And did the person who received it ever express offence or lodge a complaint?" Sammy inquired, her tone professional yet curious.

"No, nothing like that. And to be honest, it was sent three years before I was locked up," El Chapo responded, exhaling deeply as he leaned back in his chair.

"So, they simply discovered this photo on your phone during their investigation?" she asked, raising an eyebrow.

"Yes, that's correct," El Chapo replied, crossing his arms defensively.

"Was this found on your work phone or your personal phone?" she pressed further.

"It was my personal phone; I had accumulated seven years' worth of data on it. All they managed to dig up to allege any misconduct was this one picture and one text. I have a life outside of work, and I've never participated in any WhatsApp groups that share that kind of content. To only uncover two outdated messages is an absurd stretch; they're aiming at this because they lack any substantial evidence against me regarding the theft allegations," he explained, frustration seeping through his words.

In subsequent sessions, they delved into more serious claims against him, particularly an accusation that he hosted a birthday party in violation of COVID-19 restrictions and consumed alcohol while on duty.

"How many guests attended the party?" Sammy asked, her tone serious.

"There were eleven family members present. We made sure to socially distance ourselves in the garden to adhere to the guidelines. It was my 40th birthday celebration on 15th June 2020. The investigator even found the party video on my phone; if you watch it, you can clearly see us maintaining our distance," he informed her, his expression a mix of indignation and disbelief.

"And who organised the party?" Sammy continued, taking notes.

"My wife did," he responded, a note of pride evident in his voice. He then added with a chuckle,

"That's why I've taken to calling myself El Chapo. It's similar to how Tony Long was labeled the Metropolitan Police Serial Killer despite only doing his job lawfully. I haven't committed any criminal acts, nor have I engaged in gross misconduct," his laughter hung in the air, but Sammy could sense an underlying current of anger and frustration just beneath the surface.

Their next session unfolded in the tropical paradise of Barbados, where Sammy lay serenely in her hammock, swaying gently in the warm breeze.

"Is that the soothing sound of the ocean I hear in the background?" he asked, his voice filled with curiosity.

"Yes, it's incredibly relaxing here," Sammy replied, her eyes sparkling as she took in the idyllic scenery.

"Sounds divine," he responded, a smile evident in his tone, as if he could almost feel the tranquil energy surrounding her.

"It rained last night—one of those heavy downpours that leaves the world smelling fresh and alive," she explained, a hint of nostalgia in her voice. "But it twisted the hammock, and when I lay back in it earlier, it flipped me around unexpectedly, sending me tumbling to the floor. I hit my legs on a wooden table on the way down. It's quite a long way down when you're horizontal! I felt like such a fool," she admitted, a light-hearted laugh escaping her lips.

"Oh no! Are you alright?" he asked, concern lacing his voice as he pictured her tumble.

"Yes, I'm fine," she assured him, though a playful grimace passed over her face. "I've just got some rather charming bruises all over my legs now."

"Fine as in Fucked up, Insecure, Needy, and Emotional!" he chuckled, the warmth of his laughter punctuating the air.

"So, tell me about the allegations of drinking on duty," Sammy said, her curiosity piqued, eager to delve into the controversy surrounding him.

"In April 2021, a surveillance team shadowed my wife and me to the pub," he began, bewilderment creeping into his voice. "They snapped photos of me supposedly sipping a glass of wine, but it was just one tiny taste of my wife's drink. I was actually enjoying lemonade; her wine was just awful—I don't like Rosé at all. I was driving, with my pregnant wife beside me. Do you really think I would jeopardise my wife's and unborn child's safety by drinking and driving? I wasn't on duty; I was merely on call. I'm allowed to have a drink while on call as long as I'm fit for duty. They were filming me, so why didn't they simply pull me over and breathalyse me? If they thought I was unfit to drive, they should have intervened. In fact, if they suspected I was unfit and didn't stop me, they breached their own duty. There's no evidence to suggest I was drunk or unfit for work. I wasn't even arrested until September—five long months after the surveillance," he explained, his disbelief palpable as he recounted the events.

"Wow! It seems you've really ruffled some feathers; I can only imagine the staggering amount it must have cost to arrange such extensive surveillance," Sammy exclaimed, his eyes widening with intrigue. "Just think about all the expenses tied to that operation, not to mention the process of securing authorisation under the Regulation of Investigatory Powers Act (RIPA).

As for El Chapo, he went through a total of 30 counselling sessions, a lifeline during a tumultuous time. *Sapper Support* generously footed the bill after No Duff U.K. was no longer in a position to approve the funds. Their therapeutic alliance in this healing journey came to an end on August 4, 2022, marking a significant chapter's close."

Sammy collated her total client hours for the year 2021. She had worked with 39 clients over 390 sessions.

Chapter 25

Barbados Welcome Stamp 2022

Sammy had been vaccinated three times and had made a concerted effort to distance herself from the residents in her apartment complex who were grappling with mental health challenges. Now, she was eagerly planning her year in the sun-kissed paradise of Barbados.

Whenever the pressures of the day became overwhelming, her mind would drift to the idyllic beach house she had secured for her stay.

Nestled just a few meters from the sparkling Atlantic Ocean in St. Joseph on the eastern coast, "Orange Sunrise" captivated with its vibrant exterior—a warm, lively orange hue that stood out against the sky. The charming wooden house perched gracefully on stilts featured a winding staircase painted in cheerful shades of blue and yellow, leading up to a spacious deck that beckoned with promises of relaxation. There, a colourful hammock swayed gently, inviting her to unwind and bask in the soothing ocean breeze.

Inside, the house offered three well sized bedrooms: two nestled on the ground floor and the charming main bedroom perched on the mezzanine level, where natural light danced through white wooden shutters framing the windows. The staircase leading to this private retreat was adorned in whimsical blue and yellow, enhancing the house's playful character.

Sammy had confidently paid three months' rent upfront and envisioned renting a car for the first two weeks. After that, she planned to buy one, believing that this three-month period would provide ample time to figure out whether to embrace a year here or explore other enchanting locations. Each detail of her new adventure felt like a page waiting to be written in the vibrant story of her life.

Her flight was scheduled for 17th January 2022, and anticipation bubbled within her like a pot about to boil over. It had been far too long since her last escape—eight long years since she had flown abroad and she was utterly drained.

The work of counselling, though deeply rewarding, had left her emotionally spent. Day after day, she carried the stories and struggles of up to seven clients, each one a heavy stone added to her burden. The pandemic had transformed her world into a chaotic storm; she had faced the harsh realities of sexual harassment, victimisation, bullying, slander, and the looming shadow of a court case.

In the midst of that relentless turmoil, she longed for peace—a moment to breathe, to recharge, and to reclaim her joy. She deserved this break, a chance to heal and rediscover herself away from the trials that had become her everyday reality.

Chris's message blinked onto her phone screen, buzzing with excitement. "Not long to go! Maybe I'll come down and join you!"

Her heart lifted at the thought. "That would be lovely! Are you vaccinated?" she texted back, a hint of concern lacing her words.

"Absolutely. Are you still planning to work?" he inquired, his curiosity evident.

"Yes, but I'll be operating on a schedule five hours behind UK time—same time zone as you! I'll have to rise with the dawn, but that's my usual routine, so it doesn't faze me. Just fingers crossed that the internet holds up out there; if it doesn't, I'm really in trouble," she replied, a sense of apprehension curling in her stomach.

Chris's tone shifted to something more serious. "I think you're incredibly brave for heading out there alone, Samantha. I know you can take care of yourself, but please be cautious. The world has changed since the pandemic, and mental health issues are a real concern. Remember, you're going to a third world country."

Samantha felt warmth at his concern. "I know. I'll be careful. I've got my police buddies to lean on if I need advice, Chris. But I truly appreciate you looking out for me," she assured him, her heart swelling with gratitude.

With a teasing note, he brought up a familiar character. "Won't your eccentric queer Irish neighbour miss you?"

She chuckled at the memory. "He went back to Ireland, and I haven't heard from him in months," she informed him, a hint of sadness creeping into her voice.

"Bummer!" Chris replied, and she could almost hear the playful tone in his voice.

Sammy couldn't contain her laughter any longer. "Is that an American term?"

"Yes, why do you ask?"

"It's not something you often hear in the UK," she mused, her thoughts briefly drifting to the notorious figure of El Chapo— and his infamous "puff" comment — an oddly striking contrast to the lighthearted banter they had been sharing.

"Are those insufferable fools at the concierge still giving you trouble? I wish I could be in the UK right now; I would confront them directly. Men who resort to bullying women are anything but real men; they're just pathetic little boys trapped in aging bodies—and these guys are in their 50s! It's baffling. They should be fired or taken for a stern ride, taught a lesson about respect and how to treat women properly. And you know what, Samantha? You should seriously think about suing them for emotional distress. They'd be facing not just serious criminal charges but hefty financial penalties here in the US, my friend," he texted, a sense of urgency weaving through his words.

"I will be at the right moment in the future; I am quietly building my case against them," she texted back, the screen illuminating her determined expression.

In a bold move, she sold all her furniture and her car, packing her entire life into just two suitcases and a laptop case. Each item she placed inside was a memory, a piece of her past now neatly tucked away.

On Sunday, 16th January, she gathered with Anna, Ewan, Alfie, and Mia at the local Harvester. They shared laughter and heartfelt stories over plates of food as they said their bittersweet goodbyes. It was also Anna's birthday, adding an air of celebration to the day that made their farewell even more poignant.

That afternoon, she arrived at The Queens Hotel in Bournemouth. As she stepped into her lavish suite, she was captivated by the elegant decor and the stunning view from the balcony. The fresh sea breeze whispered promises of new beginnings, and she couldn't help but smile, reminding herself that she truly deserved this luxury after the trials of the past two years.

Waking early the next morning, excitement coursed through her veins. The sun was just beginning to rise, casting a golden light across the room. Her colleague from West Midlands Police was scheduled to collect her and take her to Heathrow. He arrived right on time at 7am, his cheerful demeanour matching the bright day outside. They enjoyed a hearty breakfast together in the hotel restaurant, sharing stories and good-natured banter before hitting the road.

As they drove through the waking countryside, he chuckled, "The lads just wanted to make sure you had really and truly fucked off!" His laughter filled the car, a mix of camaraderie and support as he helped her carry her bags to the departure gate, each step marking the beginning of her new journey.

"Ah bless!" She laughed out loud.

"Let me know when you arrive safely and keep in touch. I will pick you up whenever you decide to come back," he said, giving her a big hug.

Virgin Atlantic provided a wonderful experience;
their ground crew was very polite. There was a bit
of confusion since she hadn't booked a return flight.
However, after explaining that she had a "Welcome
Stamp" and was unsure about her return date, they
allowed her to check in.

The flight was on time and smooth, with no
turbulence at all. Although wearing a face mask for
eight hours felt strange, everyone complied with
COVID-19 restrictions and maintained good spirits.

Entering the country felt like stepping into a
warm embrace, the tropical air wrapping around
her as she breezed through immigration without
a hitch. As she emerged into the sun-drenched
island, the heat was palpable, prompting her to
slip off her hoodie and tuck it away in her laptop
case. The bustling airport buzzed with activity;
everyone wore masks, and hand sanitiser sat at the
entrances of every shop like a guardian of health.

Navigating through the vibrant surroundings,
she made her way to the car rental company.
With a sense of anticipation, she handed over her
documentation. Moments later, she held in her hand
a driving permit and the shiny keys to her rental
car, ready for adventure.

As she settled into her new vehicle, the horizon
was painted with the fiery hues of sunset, the
sky transitioning from gold to deep indigo. A
full moon illuminated the world around her,

casting a mesmerising glow. In the distance, she spotted a petrol station, its neon lights flickering invitingly. She drove towards it, eager to gather a few essentials. Inside, she collected milk, tea, coffee, sugar, and decadent chocolate. She planned to explore a local shop the following day for more supplies, but tonight, all she craved was a comforting cup of tea.

After a winding journey fraught with wrong turns and scenic detours, she finally arrived at "Orange Sunrise," the soft sound of waves set a serene backdrop as she was greeted by two friendly ladies who worked for the owner. They helped her with her luggage, guiding her to the fresh linen and opening the fridge to reveal a delightful surprise—well-stocked with milk, eggs, chocolate, juice, water, and even beer.

"Excellent, thank you so much!" she exclaimed, her voice tinged with gratitude as she saw them out.

Once alone, she brewed a much-needed cup of tea, the steam curling around her like a warm hug. Checking the time, she noted it was 9pm Atlantic Standard Time (AST). Weariness washed over her, the day's excitement giving way to exhaustion as she prepared to unwind in her new serene surroundings.

She unpacked her essential toiletries and nightwear, leaving the suitcases in the spare bedroom. As she climbed the stairs, she was amazed to see the biggest bed she had ever encountered. On either side of the bed were yellow bedside tables with lamps and electric fans. In the corner, there was an old green chest. The bedroom was perfect. Above the bed hung a mosquito net. Exhausted, she collapsed onto the bed and slept soundly until 3am the following morning.

Since she had clients that day, she stayed up and got dressed. The sound of the crickets chirping was enchanting, and the roar of the Atlantic was hypnotic. To her dismay, she discovered that she had been bitten during the night; those little bugs seem to get everywhere.

She sat on the deck, mesmerized by the Atlantic. Situated on the east side of the island, in a rural setting away from busy tourist areas, she could see the rough waves crashing. She was in the Scotland District of the parish of St. Joseph in Bathsheba, known as the Soup Bowl. Because of its location on the Atlantic Ocean, the waves make it one of the best surfing spots in Barbados. The tide was low in the early morning, causing the waves to crash onto the beach.

Kelly Slater, a legendary surfer celebrated around the globe, has hailed the waves at the Soup Bowl as some of his all-time favourites on Earth. This iconic spot is often regarded by scientists as home to the most consistent waves in the Caribbean, offering nearly perfect surfable conditions on almost 360 days each year. The whimsical name 'Soup Bowl' captures the essence of this breathtaking location. Coined in the 1960s, the name reflects the beauty of the curling wave that forms a perfect 'bowl,' while the frothy whitewater cascading after the wave crashes evokes the imagery of delicious 'soup.'

During the warm summer months of July and August, the waves are relatively gentle, cascading at heights of just 2-3 feet, perfect for leisurely rides. As summer gives way to fall, from September to October, the excitement builds as waves swell to a thrilling 3-6 feet. Yet, the true magic of the Soup Bowl occurs from November to April, when powerful winter swells from the north collide with distant hurricane-generated swells, unleashing colossal waves that often soar above 15 feet. This intoxicating combination of nature's forces transforms the Soup Bowl into a paradise for professional surfers, seeking the ultimate adrenaline rush amid the roaring surf.

She waited patiently for the golden rays of the sun to break over the horizon before stepping onto the warm, soft sand of the beach. Each grain felt like a small embrace under her bare feet, grounding her in tranquility. The beach was deserted, and the rhythmic crash of waves against the shore created a soothing soundtrack that wrapped around her like a comforting blanket. She settled onto the sand, stretching her legs out, and lost herself in the mesmerising dance of the sapphire waves.

Before long, a towering figure approached—a Black man, easily standing at 6 feet 2 inches. She regarded him with a hint of suspicion as he neared.

"Hey, man! I'm your neighbour," he said with an easy grin. "I live in the white property just below you. I know your landlord, Spoc man; I heard you'll be here for a year."

He plopped down next to her, invading her personal space without invitation, his presence suddenly too close for comfort.

"Oh, okay. Are you vaccinated?" Sammy asked, her voice laced with caution.

"Nah, man!" he answered with a carefree laugh, his lack of a mask evident.

"I have to go back to work. Bye," she said firmly, rising to her feet.

He trailed behind her as she made her way back to her apartment, eager to capture her attention. She manoevered carefully, striving to keep a respectful distance.

"I can get you anything you want, man—fruit, coconuts, anything!" he called after her, his bright smile lingering in the air, an oddly cheerful contrast to her unease.

"Thanks, I don't need anything," she replied, her voice steady, as she ascended the sun-soaked stairs to Orange Sunrise. For a fleeting moment, a pang of anxiety gripped her — she feared he might follow her, that his shadow would loom behind her as she sought refuge in her new home.

As the hours drifted by, she became aware of her other neighbors. They were a cheerful white couple in their forties, with laughter bubbling up from their young daughter, who danced around them with uninhibited joy. Their voices floated through the air, blending British and Canadian accents into a harmonious melody that silhouetted the warmth of their family dynamic.

The heat of the day swelled, wrapping around her like a warm blanket, prompting her to take a drive and hunt for a place to purchase a car. She aimed to find both a vehicle and some groceries. After a bit of searching, she stumbled upon a local store, but the prices were steep, biting into her budget and leaving a bitter taste in her mouth. Her quest for a car dealership, however, was met with disappointment; every lead seemed to dissolve into nothingness.

Back at the apartment, she settled into the corner where the TV stood waiting, a portal to a world beyond her own. It was equipped with Netflix and a variety of local channels. She discovered, to her delight, that she could access her Prime account, allowing her to indulge in a few episodes of "Chicago PD," as the familiar theme music filled the room, she felt the weight of her worries begin to lift, the tension unraveling like a tightly wound spring.

After unwinding with her show, she turned to her phone, searching for car sales outlets, but most appeared to be closed — a casualty of the ongoing pandemic, perhaps. Frustration building, she decided to reach out to Peggy, the woman who arranged her apartment rental. Peggy turned out to be a wellspring of invaluable information, suggesting a contact who rented out cars and sold ex-rentals. With a renewed sense of hope, Sammy scheduled an appointment to check out a Kia Rio and mentally added a printer to her to-do list, eager to set up her workspace.

The following morning, the sun peeked through the curtains of Sammy's apartment as she stepped outside, eager for a day at the beach. However, her excitement quickly turned to surprise when she nearly stumbled over three large coconuts that lay haphazardly on the steps, their rough, fibrous shells glistening in the early sunlight. Shaking off the distraction, she continued her walk, the sound of the ocean waves now calling her.

Out of the corner of her eye, she spotted Terry, the guy from the neighbouring white property, approaching her yet again.

"Hey, my name is Terry, man! I left you some coconuts outside this morning. I can get you fruits and all kinds of things if you need, just let me know," he said, his voice rich with a Bajan lilt.

Sammy considered her errands for the day. She needed to visit the car rental place to inspect a vehicle and track down a printer. The thought of navigating a foreign island without a sat nav weighed on her; the exorbitant cost of data in Barbados was a daunting consideration. Plus, she wanted to pick up a cheap phone to help her stay connected.

"Okay, do you know where Christchurch is? I need to check out a car there this morning. Also, do you know where I can find a printer and a phone?" she inquired, her curiosity mingling with a sense of urgency.

"Yeah, man, I can come with you! What time are you leaving? Just put my number in your phone," he offered enthusiastically, a wide grin spreading across his face.

With a nod, Sammy entered his number into her phone and quickly texted him her own. She instructed him to meet her by her car at 9am, hoping it would make the day's daunting tasks a little easier.

The sun was already scorching the asphalt as he arrived right on time, sliding into the passenger seat of her vehicle. Sammy handed him a spare mask, her voice firm yet polite. "Please wear a mask." Terry obliged, though, in a way that made her heart race unexpectedly—he rested his leg against hers, a casual but startling intrusion of personal space.

Feeling a flush of discomfort, she shifted slightly and said, "Uh, could you move your leg off mine, please?"

"I can't help having long legs, man!" he replied, laughing lightly, though Sammy couldn't help but feel a twinge of unease at the playful lack of regard for boundaries.

They ventured to a bustling commercial outlet park in Christchurch, where she carefully selected a sleek printer and filled up her cart with an array of fresh groceries. After her shopping spree, he guided her to the car rental facility, where she examined the shiny vehicle with keen interest before taking it for a test drive. The car felt just right, and she confidently agreed on the price and set a date to collect it, which conveniently fell on the same day she would be returning the rental at the airport. They arranged for someone to pick her up from the airport in the new car, and she would then drop the driver off in Christchurch on her way back to Orange Sunrise. Everything seemed perfectly planned.

She felt an unsettling urge to distance herself from him; her instincts were buzzing, sensing something off about his demeanour. They stepped out of the car, and she headed toward the white steps.

"Thanks for your help. Goodbye," she said, trying to keep her tone light.

She collected the grocery bags, feeling the weight of her purchases in her hands, and walked up the side steps. She opened the door to the deck, then stepped into the apartment and headed straight for the fridge to put away her provisions.

To her dismay, Terry had followed her, bringing the printer along with him. He had placed it casually on a chair and perched himself onto the deck sofa, propping his feet up as if it were his personal lounge. He plugged his phone into a nearby socket and began rolling a spliff, completely unaware of the discomfort he was causing her.

"Oh my God, no!" She thought.

"You need to leave now!" she declared firmly.

"Nah, man, I ain't leavin'. Get me a beer!" he demanded, his tone defiant.

Sammy was taken aback. "No, you have to leave—this is non-negotiable," she shot back, locking her eyes onto his.

To her dismay, he lit the spliff and took a long drag, glaring at her as he smirked. "Get me a beer!"

Sammy recalled the machete resting on top of the fridge, prepared for any situation.

"As a former police officer, I will not tolerate that on my rental property. You need to leave immediately," she stated with unwavering authority.

He stood up, holding her gaze. She could see the effects of the drug taking hold, and his grin transformed into something menacing that chilled her to the bone.

"At least you ain't aggressive, man," with that, he exited.

Sammy paused in the kitchen, allowing herself a moment to think. She took the machete from the top of the fridge and laid it on the kitchen surface. It was rusty, but she knew what to do with it if necessary. Just as she settled into the comforting stillness, her phone buzzed with a photograph of him, a spliff dangling carelessly from his lips. Frustrated, she hurriedly typed a message, demanding that he leave her alone.

The days that followed felt like an eternity as she scanned her surroundings for any sign of him, but he remained conspicuously absent. Seeking solace, she strolled along the sun-kissed beach, the soft sand squishing beneath her toes. It was there that she encountered her neighbors from the nearby Blue Lagoon, a welcoming sight amidst the solitude.

"Hi, how are you? We're Rachel and Andy, and this is our daughter, Nevaeh," Rachel said, her bright smile radiating kindness.

"Sammy, pleased to meet you all," she replied, feeling a sense of relief wash over her.

"Are you here on your own?" Rachel inquired, her eyes sparkling with curiosity.

"Yes, I have the twelve-month welcome stamp," Sammy answered, a hint of pride in her voice.

"So do we! We've been here since November. Isn't it beautiful? We arrived after living in Africa; we work as missionaries," Rachel shared, her enthusiasm palpable as she gestured to the azure waves lapping at the shore.

"Wow, that sounds incredible," Sammy responded, genuinely impressed by their adventurous spirit.

"But be cautious of the man in the white house below us. He's a drug addict and swindled us out of money. He promised to bring us fresh fruit, and we handed him ten dollars, but he never showed. I can even smell the drugs wafting from that house," Rachel warned, her expression turning serious.

"Yes, I've encountered him. I told him to get lost," Sammy replied, a mix of relief and resolve in her voice.

"Hey! Do you want to join us for dinner later?" Rachel asked, her voice bright with enthusiasm.

"Oh wow, that sounds amazing! Thank you!" Sammy replied, her eyes lighting up with excitement.

"Come over at 6pm," Rachel instructed with a warm smile.

"Thanks so much! I'll see you later," Sammy responded, feeling a swell of gratitude.

Rachel radiated kindness.

When Sammy arrived punctually at the Blue Lagoon, she was greeted by the warm glow of the setting sun reflecting off the water; it was beautiful. The evening unfolded into a delightful gathering with Rachel, Andy, and Neveah. Rachel, a Canadian native with an infectious laugh, had once worked as an Emergency Medical Technician (EMT), while Andy, a ruggedly charming carpenter from Norfolk in the UK, had an easygoing demeanour.

As they settled in, Rachel opened up about the distressing tale of the previous tenant at Orange Sunrise. He had been victimised by Terry's relentless harassment, theft, and intimidation. The poor man had suffered a stroke and had to endure a painful hospitalisation.

"Could you help me look for his clothes?" Rachel asked, her brow furrowed in concern. "He left a suit hanging in the wardrobe and asked us to collect it for him when we have a chance."

"Oh my God, that's awful! Is he okay now?" Sammy exclaimed, her heart aching for the man as she scratched her head in disbelief.

"He flew home, but we have his address. At least we can reach out to him," Andy chimed in, his voice steady but laced with empathy.

"If Terry bothers me again, I'm going to the police. This kind of behaviour needs to stop," Sammy asserted, a fierce determination in her eyes.

As days turned into months, the bond between them blossomed. They shared countless joyful moments—laughing on sun-drenched beach days, whipping up decadent cookies and creamy milkshakes in the kitchen, and curling up with captivating books on the deck under the shade of swaying palm trees. Andy, a passionate surfer, became a source of inspiration as the girls cheered him on while he rode the crashing waves, his figure silhouetted against the vibrant sky. They exchanged heartfelt stories of their experiences as first responders, reminiscing about the challenges of the pandemic, and embracing the simple joys of everyday life together.

Chapter 26

District F

On Friday 28th January, she returned her hire car at the bustling airport, the scent of jet fuel mingling with the hot morning air. After handing over the keys, she returned to her trusted Kia Rio — a vibrant little car that felt like safety on wheels. She dropped the driver with Katrina at the rental company and drove back to the quiet embrace of Orange Sunrise. The sun dipped low, painting the sky with tired golds, and she looked forward to solitude.

Her phone buzzed. A text from Terry.
"Nice car."

Annoyance flared hot in her chest. She had forgotten to block him. With one swift movement she did, erasing his access to her life.

On Monday 31st January, the day after her birthday, she walked into District F Police Station in St. Joseph. The fluorescent lights hummed overhead. She showed Officer Ali the picture Terry had sent her — smoke curling around him — and

the follow-up message where she had demanded
he leave her alone. She explained that he had been
watching her and texted her after she told him to
leave her alone.

Ali studied the phone, his face set. He admitted
Terry was known to them. His tone was clipped,
authoritative, leaving no space for question: "Drive
back to your apartment. I'll follow."

So she did. He followed in a marked car, another
police vehicle joining in. Blue lights sliced through
the afternoon. The show of force rattled her nerves.

At Orange Sunrise, Ali and the others confronted
Terry. When he returned to her, Ali said flatly that
Terry denied harassment and claimed she had
approached him. Her stomach dropped.

She stood tall, her voice sharp with truth: "A
woman of my calibre would never associate with
someone like him, or allow drugs in my home."

Ali's reply was casual, dismissive. "Da man been
cussing out women on da street. He ignorant, ya
know."

Then, abruptly, he gave her his personal mobile
number. "Call me anytime."

It was a breach — she didn't see it then, but this was
the first line crossed. He wasn't meant to blur the
uniform with personal invitations. But she was a

lone tourist, isolated, desperate for reassurance. She saved the number.

The next day, 1st February, his police car appeared outside her home. No call first. No reason given. He knocked, loudly.

She was mid-session with a client from Merseyside Police. She wrapped up quickly, embarrassed, and opened the door.

"Samantha, are you in?" His voice carried authority.

She told him to come in, and he stepped onto her deck, settling himself as though he belonged there. Then he pressed, "Why haven't you called me? Would you like to do something on Saturday?"

It sounded casual. Friendly. But his presence, uninvited, felt heavy. The uniform blurred into something personal, and she felt the conflict inside her — he was a police officer, she was alone in a foreign country, and saying no didn't feel simple.

She mentioned it to Rachel and Andrew later. She dressed it as reassurance, that a local officer was "keeping an eye out," but the truth was, he had already crossed a line.

That Saturday, 5th February, he arrived again. Not for duty. Not for safety. For her. She let him in, feeling obliged, boxed in by the trust she thought she was supposed to place in the Police.

They drove the East Coast Road. The scenery was glorious but his presence felt invasive, the conversation circling back to him. At KFC, he introduced her as his wife to the cashier. A "joke," she laughed politely, but the words jarred — too familiar, too claiming.

Over greasy food he talked of children by different women, about living alone. It wasn't warmth; it was disarming disclosure, an attempt to fold her into his world quickly. She listened, but unease curled in her stomach.

By the time he dropped her home, she was drained. He lingered, telling her she should move to Barbados permanently. She smiled faintly, thanked him, and closed the door. Relief washed over her.

The next day he arrived again, unannounced, carrying food. This time, in her kitchen, he kissed her neck without invitation. It was swift, presumptuous. She froze. He pulled back with a grin, promising to call later. And from then on, he did — daily. Visits, calls, texts. The pressure wrapped itself around her life like vines.

He invited her to the station, into the front office during his night shifts, into his car. Every gesture blurred professional duty with personal intrusion. It was grooming. But she couldn't yet see it.

She was a woman alone, a tourist, and he wore the uniform of safety.

By March, he told her he loved her. He wanted to marry her. Her laugh was nervous, uncertain. *We hardly know each other.* But already she was entangled, her boundaries eroded. He had moved too fast, on purpose.

This was never romance. It was control, dressed up as care.

Chapter 27

Is this World War III?

By March 2022 the world felt unstable. News of Ukraine filled the airwaves, and each headline pressed heavier on her chest. The talk of escalation, of war spreading west, left her cold with fear. She had already been carrying too much, and the thought of World War III breaking out while she was stranded in the Caribbean made the decision for her. She would go home.

She told Ali. He sat across from her, the uniform that should have been reassurance now something else entirely. She said she was flying on 17th March. He leaned back, studied her, and then told her to leave her car with him. He offered to sell it, to "keep the money safe," he insisted. It was framed as help, but it carried weight. Refusing didn't feel like an option.

On 16th March, the afternoon before her flight, he drove her out to his property. A sprawling house, animals wandering, trophies lined up — he paraded it before her like proof of status. He wanted her to see what he owned, what he could offer. He told stories of protecting Tony Blair, of guarding Fidel Castro, of being the police martial arts champion. It was grand, exaggerated, the kind of boasting she had heard from men before.

But here, alone, dependent on his "help," she didn't challenge him. She smiled thinly, let him talk. Inside, her gut told her it was all performance.

That evening he took her to a hotel near the airport. At the pool, with the sun bleeding out over the horizon, he carried on with the stories — building himself up, inflating his power. She sat beside him, quiet, already thinking about her flight home, her court case in April, the relief of escape.

Later, on the beach, under the moon, he pressed close. He rubbed his face against hers, not tenderly but like a claim. His voice was thick when he asked, "When will I see you again?"

She gave him the only answer that would move things along. *"After my court case. You have my car. You have my money. I'll be back,"* the words weren't a promise of love. They were a placation, a way to ease herself out of his grip.

On 17th March, the plane cut through the clouds and lifted her away from Barbados. Relief spread cold through her veins. Home was waiting, even if it was cold, even if it was empty.

Her apartment was bare, no furniture, no comfort. That first night she lay in the bath, wrapped in towels, shivering in the absence of warmth. But it was hers. It was England. It was away from him.

Within weeks she was building again: a bed, a home, a black Audi TT Quattro that lifted her spirit each time the engine growled to life. Andy "Otis" Reading's voice echoed in her mind — "Fire up the Quattro!" — and she laughed, a sound born of resilience.

Back to life. Back to reality. Back to the here and now.

Chapter 28

Civil Court, The BACP Farce & Dorset Police

In April, she participated in a Civil Court hearing via a Zoom session involving LMG Design Ltd. The verdict was in her favour; he lost the case, which meant she was relieved from the obligation of settling his outstanding invoice.

"Just go away, you ridiculous little boy!" she muttered to herself in frustration.

Following this court outcome, she reached out to her insurance company for assistance, which promptly provided her with a barrister to help navigate the ongoing BACP complaint.

Debbie Downer, a key figure in this dispute, had sent a statement to the British Association for Counselling and Psychotherapy (BACP) claiming she was a client of Sammy's. This was a blatant falsehood. When the BACP reviewed her statement, Debbie insisted that Sammy had "engaged with her in a counselling manner," however, when BACP representatives probed further for evidence, asking for a copy of her counselling service contract and proof of payment for any sessions, Debbie stumbled and claimed that Sammy had offered her free counselling. This assertion was entirely untrue; Sammy, having dedicated seven rigorous years to her training, was well aware of her professional value and would never compromise her worth by providing complimentary services.

It became increasingly clear that Debbie Downer, much like her husband, was not only unreliable but fundamentally dishonest, and her testimony could not be trusted as a credible account of events.

Sammy had unraveled the tangled web of her situation after facing a dead end with Phoenix Heroes. In a calculated move, she joined forces with DFSB Ltd and discovered they had similarly floundered in their complaint to the BACP, as they were not deemed clients. Undeterred, she resorted to deception, falsely claiming to the BACP that she indeed was a client. To bolster her position, Sammy meticulously compiled her client log and supervision records, which unequivocally demonstrated that Debbie Downer was never a client.

In an unexpected twist, the BACP, in a decision that left Sammy, her supervisor, and her counselling colleagues aghast, announced it would convene a practice review hearing. To Sammy's horror, they planned to summon Debbie Downer as a witness.

A wave of disbelief washed over Sammy. How could the BACP entertain the testimony of a witness who had already been shown to be dishonest?

Adding to her frustration, her paralegal displayed an unsettling indifference, leaving Sammy feeling disillusioned. It felt as if her paralegal were somehow aligned with the BACP's stance. In response, Sammy poured her heart into a statement meticulously outlining the toxic and malicious nature of the complaint, as well as the fraught history of her civil dispute with Sleazy. However, her paralegal dismissed these critical details, asserting they were irrelevant. Sammy shot back, passionately insisting that they were, in fact, highly relevant; after all, Debbie Downer had never been a client, and her complaint was nothing but a vexatious ploy.

"What exactly am I being accused of?" Sammy demanded, her voice tinged with frustration as she confronted the paralegal on the other end of the line. The paralegal's tone dripped with condescension, as if speaking to a child, which only fuelled Sammy's irritation. "None of the ethical frameworks apply here; she isn't my client. This is a civil matter, and her complaint is nothing more than a vexatious nuisance."

The paralegal, unimpressed, replied, "The BACP believes you have brought them into disrepute by diagnosing both the complainant and her husband."

Firing back, Sammy retorted with a fierce determination, "I did not diagnose anyone."

"But you did write in your counterclaim that she was suicidal and her husband was depressed," the paralegal stated, her tone matter-of-fact yet heavy with implication.

"She was threatening to throw herself off the balcony," Sammy replied, a hint of frustration creeping into her voice. "You don't need to be a psychiatrist to see that she was exhibiting suicidal ideation. And her husband? He confided in me that the weight of losing his income during the pandemic was crushing him. He was working in my home, trying to make ends meet. My counterclaim clearly outlines that I offered him this job out of kindness, hoping to alleviate their financial strain," she continued, her passion evident.

"The BACP will post the outcome on their website," the paralegal continued, "and if you choose not to attend the hearing, they'll still go ahead and reveal the results without you there."

"Let them," Sammy replied defiantly, her resolve hardening.

In the following days, Sammy found herself immersed in a gathering with her supervisor and a group of counsellors who had banded together to form a support network, united in their experiences with the BACP. The room buzzed with voices, each counsellor voicing their opinion that the BACP were bringing itself into disrepute for bringing a practice review hearing against Sammy that was evidently vexatious.

The practice review started with the barrister representing the BACP giving her a filthy look.

"Jeez Louise, he is as childish as the rest of them," Sammy thought to herself, smiling at him sweetly.

"You have brought the BACP into disrepute by trying to influence the judge in the court case with the complainant's husband," he lorded it over her.

Sammy, feeling a rush of defiance, interjected, "Did you obtain a witness statement from the judge who presided over the hearing?"

"Uh, well, no," he snapped, caught off guard.

"There is no evidence that I influenced his decision in any way," she declared with fierce conviction, her eyes narrowing as she faced the panel. "I dedicated five years to rigorous training with the Counselling and Psychotherapy Central Awarding Body (CPCAB), and it was under the guidance of my training provider that I chose to become a member of your esteemed organisation. Surely, this membership entitles me to proudly display your logo and list my membership details after my name, does it not?"

Her gaze pierced through the room, a glare full of defiance. "The general public never had, nor will ever have, access to my counterclaim; it was strictly a private court document. Likewise, the email I sent to the complainant's husband was confidential and intended solely for him. It is not I who have thrust this matter into the public spotlight—it is the complainant herself who has done so. Thus, I stand resolutely convinced that I have not brought the BACP into any disrepute."

With a decisive breath, she pressed on, "The evidence to which you refer was merely a counterclaim document seen exclusively by the Bournemouth court. I signed it with my usual flourish, proudly adding 'Member of the BACP' beneath my signature. Frankly, I doubt the judge is even familiar with your organisation," she concluded, her voice steady as she reclaimed her composure amidst the rising tension.

The hearing lasted two hours. Debbie Downer provided her evidence, looking miserable and playing the victim, presenting herself in a child ego state. After an hour of deliberation, the panel returned with their verdict.

Case not proven.

"Go away, you silly little girl!" she thought to herself.

She decided to cancel her membership and
seek refuge with The National Counselling &
Psychotherapy Society, drawn in by its significantly
lower fees. With newfound financial relief, she also
made the switch to a different insurance provider,
discontented by the lacklustre legal team her
previous insurer had assigned to her. The new
policy not only lightened her financial burden but
also brought a welcome sense of renewal. Every
cloud truly has its silver lining.

Following her barrister's prudent advice to remain
calm and composed, she chose not to provoke the
situation with Debbie Downer and Sleazy during
the tense practice review investigation and the
subsequent hearing. Now, as the dust began
to settle, she felt a surge of freedom, igniting
her resolve to pursue the justice she so rightly
deserved.

In the dim light of her office, she penned a letter to
LMG Design Ltd, meticulously outlining her request
for copies of all their communications, as well as
every quote and invoice relating to the botched
work performed at her home. With a determined
sigh, she sealed the envelope and slipped it through
his door, the sound of paper rustling echoing in the
stillness. Despite her efforts, he chose to ignore
her, prompting her to reach out to the Information
Commissioner's Office once more. Following their
guidance, she sent a Subject Access Request, firmly
giving him a deadline of 30 days to respond.

Frustration turned to resolve as she filed a claim for £7,000 against him, bolstered by quotes from local builders eager to remedy the shoddy craftsmanship. Her kitchen sink, a perpetual source of annoyance, continued to leak, poorly fitted and too small for the gaping hole that would forever mock her attempts at home improvement. In the en-suite bathroom, he had carelessly slathered plumbers' putty over the exposed pipes, but the result was disastrous: a grotesque drip had marred the beautiful cabinetry, leaving it sticky and unusable—a sight that filled her with despair. Determining whether the pipes or sink were damaged seemed a Herculean task, one that would undoubtedly involve costly repairs, each layer of the mystery deepening as she contemplated the nightmare ahead. The sealant in the en-suite had cracked dramatically, a jagged line that traced the divide between the tiles and the ceiling, hinting at the underlying problems hidden from view. Even the wardrobe doors hung askew, while the luxurious karndean flooring lay inconsistently fitted, a testament to the man's lack of skill.

To fortify her case, she gathered quotations from two reputable builders and packaged them with video evidence, arranging everything meticulously for the court.

Just a few days later, the calm was shattered by a firm knock on her door. Startled, she opened it to find two officers standing on her porch, their expressions serious and unreadable.

"We are here to address an allegation of harassment made by your neighbours," one of the officers stated, his voice steady but laden with the weight of the situation. The words hung in the air like an ominous cloud, casting a new shadow over Sammy's already complicated life.

With a mix of frustration and determination, Sammy recounted her side of the story, eager to clarify that she was not harassing anyone—she was merely trying to resolve issues regarding her property. She laid out her documentary evidence, each piece a testament to her innocence.

The officer then delivered the surprising news: Debbie Downer had claimed to them that she was a client of Sammy's.

"What? That's absurd! She is not a client and is clearly lying to you! You should charge her with wasting police time!" Sammy exclaimed, disbelief and anger rising in her voice.

"She has filed a witness statement asserting her status as a client and stating that as her counsellor, you should know that the letters you've sent would cause her harassment, alarm, and distress," the officer explained, his tone remaining professional but firm. "She's a liar," Sammy retorted, her eyes flashing with indignation.

"They seem assertive to me, not harassing," he replied with a small smile, attempting to diffuse the tension. The officers left, satisfied that no crimes had occurred, but the unease lingered in the air.

Determined to seek justice, Sammy wrote once again to the Information Commissioners Office (ICO), informing them that LMG Design Ltd had failed to respond to her Subject Access Request (SAR).

The ICO took action by contacting LMG Design Ltd and subsequently fining them for not being properly registered. In a flurry of activity, they provided all the required documentation to Sammy shortly thereafter. A date for a preliminary Zoom hearing at Bournemouth Civil Court was set, and she found herself facing Sleazy, who sat across from her, his expression a storm of suppressed fury as if he might erupt at any moment.

She stood before the judge, her voice steady yet tinged with frustration, recounting how the police had come to her after Sleazy lodged a complaint against her for harassment. As she spoke, the weight of his wife's deceit hung heavy in the air; she had spun a web of lies that ensnared various organisations, including Phoenix Heroes, the BACP, DFSB Ltd, HCS Cleaning Services Ltd, PMB Property Management, Directions Property, Dorset Police, and even the residents of her apartment complex. These insidious tales had spread like wildfire, tarnishing her reputation.

Sammy detailed the countless hurdles Sleazy had put in her way regarding paperwork. When she finally received the invoices, she was astounded to find that they lacked VAT, casting doubt on his registered VAT status. Even more perplexing, his quotation letters bore the name of an entirely different business, while the invoices were printed on letterhead that seemed to belong to a different realm altogether. The discrepancies were glaring; the quotes and invoices clashed like mismatched puzzle pieces.

To top it off, the bank details he provided for payment led to his personal account rather than a legitimate business account, further deepening the confusion. None of it added up, and the tangled mess left her bewildered. The judge, sharp and perceptive, saw through Sleazy's web of deception and delivered a powerful reprimand that reverberated through the courtroom. It was a moment of clarity and justice, a beautiful sight that brought a sense of relief and vindication.

"The police have more pressing matters to focus on than your complaints of harassment; you have not been harassed. The complainant is fully entitled to request information from you in writing. We will proceed to trial, you will receive an email with the scheduled date shortly."

The Information Commissioners Office (ICO) reached out to DFSB Ltd to address serious concerns regarding their lack of compliance.

In a firm yet informative letter, they issued a warning, emphasising the importance of taking necessary steps to rectify the situation and align with regulatory standards. In a bid to gather intelligence, they also recorded her complaint not only against DFSB Ltd but also against HCS Cleaning Services, which was notably not affiliated with the ICO.

In response to the troubling situation, she took to the internet to express her thoughts, crafting detailed reviews of all the companies involved, including PMB Property Management. With every word she wrote, a fierce conviction echoed in her mind: "The truth will out."

Chapter 29

BetterHelp.com

During her time in Barbados, she was approached by BetterHelp.com, a prominent online therapy platform that specialises in providing mental health support. BetterHelp connects individuals seeking therapy with licensed professionals through a seamless and intuitive online platform, allowing users to communicate via text, chat, and phone calls. Established in 2013 in Los Angeles, BetterHelp has become a leading resource for those looking to access mental health services from the comfort of their own homes.

After being recruited, she participated in a thorough online interview process where she demonstrated her qualifications and expertise in therapy. Following the successful interview, she submitted all necessary documentation and was delighted to receive an offer to work as a self-employed therapist for BetterHelp.

Her journey as a therapist with BetterHelp began in May when she took on her first client. By the end of the year, she had made significant strides in her practice, working with 61 clients in total and accumulating an impressive 471 hours of counselling experience. This opportunity not only allowed her to help numerous individuals on their mental health journeys but also enabled her to grow professionally in a dynamic and supportive online environment.

Chapter 30

PTSD & Suicide Awareness Training

Stew Henderson, a dedicated member of The Diplomatic & Parliamentary Protection Group, reached out to her to discuss his important role as the Veterans Lead for the Metropolitan Police. A former soldier in the Scots Guards, Stew carries with him a deep-seated pride in his service, which fuels his unwavering commitment to support veterans in need.

Many veterans grapple with the invisible wounds of undiagnosed PTSD, which can manifest in a powerful array of emotions and behaviours. Tragically, these struggles often push them to the brink, leading some to fall through the cracks of society, confronting battles with depression, thoughts of suicide, homelessness, and even criminality. Stew's heartfelt mission is to illuminate these hidden challenges and provide the necessary support to prevent such outcomes.

They engaged in an in-depth discussion about her training courses, a conversation filled with enthusiasm and shared experiences. Stew, along with several other dedicated officers, embraced the opportunity to undertake the training course via Zoom, adapting to the virtual format with remarkable resilience. His evaluation form came back glowing with positivity, reflecting not only his commitment to the training but also the valuable insights he gained. Eager to share his progress, he relayed details of the course and the impactful work he was doing to his partner, Cemal, who listened intently, nodding in support.

Months later, a sense of purpose led Cemal to reach out to Sammy with a special request. He inquired if she would be willing to nominate Stewart for the prestigious King's Police Medal. The request carried a solemn sense of confidentiality, needing to remain a secret even from the unsuspecting Stewart.

Motivated by her admiration for Stew's dedication and bravery, Sammy took pen to paper, crafting a heartfelt nomination letter addressed to the King, filled with genuine appreciation for Stewart's extraordinary contributions to his community and the police force.

A dedicated firearms officer from Merseyside, who had recently completed the intensive training course, shared glowing feedback about Sammy with a colleague in Cheshire Constabulary. This connection followed a period of significant change, as Cheshire had merged seamlessly with North Wales Police to form a new entity known as the North West Alliance.

Shortly thereafter, Sammy was approached by a sergeant from the Dog Section. The urgent call came after a constable in that unit tragically took his own life, leaving behind a haunting void and an overwhelming sense of grief within the constabulary. Recognising the profound effects of this tragedy, the sergeant recommended Sammy as a compassionate counsellor, reaching out to support several officers grappling with their emotions in the aftermath of such a loss.

In March 2025, a sergeant and two inspectors from the North West Alliance Firearms Unit and Dog Section participated in a PTSD Awareness training session tailored for law enforcement officers and first responders, conducted via Zoom.

The course was met with enthusiasm and appreciation, as participants recognised the importance of mental health awareness. Plans were quickly set in motion to ensure that 140 officers received this vital training in PTSD Awareness and further training in Suicide Awareness for Law Enforcement Officers, empowering them with tools and knowledge essential for navigating the challenges they faced in the line of duty.

On the day of the Borough Market terrorist attacks, Stewart Henderson found himself amidst the chaos of London. With an unwavering presence of mind, he sprang into action, prioritising public safety in the face of panic. He skilfully relayed vital information to SCO19, ensuring those in authority could respond swiftly. Amidst the turmoil, he sought out victims, offering crucial support, administering first aid with remarkable composure. His acts of bravery and valour shone brightly in a time of darkness, showcasing his remarkable courage and commitment to helping others.

Stewart found himself deeply entrenched in the demanding and often harrowing work of being the Metropolitan Police Armed Forces Lead, and being associated with Veterans charities in the UK. His commitment was not only time-consuming but also emotionally taxing, as he devoted countless hours to this vital cause during his personal time. This dedication connected him with Scotty Caswell, the Armed Forces Lead of Warwickshire Police. In May, Scotty reached out to Sammy, eager to explore the possibility of training sessions focused on the critical issues of PTSD and Suicide Awareness, aiming to equip himself with the knowledge and skills to make a meaningful impact.

Scotty enthusiastically presented Sammy with an extensive list of 43 Police Armed Forces Leads from across the UK. Each entry was meticulously detailed, featuring names, ranks, and specific departments or units. This treasure trove of information was sure to provide opportunities for Sammy to educate key personnel across the UK so they, in turn, could help veterans who came into contact with the police.

Chapter 31

Reflections

In this world, we encounter a spectrum of humanity, ranging from dishonourable souls driven by greed, envy, and self-interest to hardworking, steadfast individuals who embody honesty and trustworthiness. The former lurk in the shadows, revelling in their own bitterness and spreading misery like a contagion, poisoning their lives with their malicious thoughts and actions.

But amidst this darkness, a beacon of hope shines in the form of dedicated individuals who embody integrity and courage. The true spirit of fidelity and bravery was undeniably evident among veterans of the Armed Forces and first responders during the harrowing times of the pandemic. Their unwavering commitment and selfless service deserve our most profound appreciation and gratitude.

Sammy, too, has faced her own tumultuous journey. Between the years 2019 and 2022, she danced precariously with the dark suicidal ideation of her

clients, grappling with despair. Yet, to the best of
her knowledge, her clients have emerged from their
battles intact, navigating toward brighter days and
a safer future.

Epilogue

Kian tenderly succumbed to cancer in 2021, his final moments spent surrounded by the warmth of home in Cavan, where he found peace.

Paws, a charming feline full of personality, found a new loving home in the picturesque surroundings of Dorset, thanks to the efforts of Cats Protection.

In a dramatic turn of events, Debbie Downer and Sleazy decided to part ways with their apartment, packing up their lives and leaving the complex behind. Their world is thick with tension as a civil court case looms over them, still pending resolution.

In a disturbing episode, Sammy experienced repeated invasions of her personal space by a persistent sexual harasser. After enduring too much, she sought help from the police, who intervened to warn him. Determined to stand up for herself, Sammy poured her feelings into a letter, demanding he leave her alone. When he replied, she chose not to engage, shoving his words into the shredder without a second glance.

Stan bid farewell to DFSB Ltd — thank God.

In January 2023, a treacherous patch of ice in the car park became Sammy's unexpected adversary, sending her tumbling and causing significant injury to her elbow. Now, she navigates the aftermath of the fall, with a civil court case against the management company on the horizon.

Mark continues to serve at DFSB Ltd, joined by several fresh faces on the staff. Together, they brighten her day by cheerfully delivering her parcels, opening doors, and greeting her with sincere smiles. The Directors remain present on-site, but Sammy chooses silence, avoiding any interaction. Thankfully, Mark has restored her access to the door that once welcomed Debbie Downer.

After a tumultuous period, the Right to Manage company made the decisive choice to fire PMB in 2022, ushering in a more professional management team focused on meeting the needs of the residents.

Phoenix Heroes and **No Duff U.K.** made the bold decision to leave the British Association for Counselling and Psychotherapy (BACP), seeking a new beginning with the National Counselling and Psychotherapy Society (NCPS). Dean Owen passionately voiced his discontent, arguing that the BACP had devolved into a profit-driven entity, neglecting the true interests of its members and failing to uphold professional standards.

In a somewhat perplexing twist, El Chapo emerged from his recent tribulations without facing criminal charges. Undeterred, he is now in the thick of an appeal regarding the disciplinary case lodged against him, fighting to clear his name.